WIND CHILL

A NOVELLA BY

PATRICK RUTIGLIANO

Crystal Lake Publishing
www.CrystalLakePub.com

FOR HANNAH

Who was quite literally there with bells on—even in
the dead of winter.

JESUS, MARY, AND JOSEPH'S *left nut!*
Eric Kinley woke up blind to the frozen world around him, but not to the grin that had followed him back from sleep. The face leered at him through the darkness behind his eyes. Pale cheeks squelched like maggots as the grin widened. The lipless mouth said nothing, the teeth inside clenching so tight the incisors cracked. Its sunken eyes lusted. The pinpoints of scarlet light at their centers roved up and down Eric's body as if measuring every inch of him. Weighing him. Slowly, the jaws began to open, stretching until the swirling darkness within shamed the surrounding black. It took a lump of snow falling into Eric's open mouth to make him realize he was awake. The visage finally receded into the blackness. He sputtered. Only the lights in the depths of the creature's eyes lingered, intensifying for just a moment before finally flickering out.

"Fucking nightmare bullshit!"

"You okay, man?"

Eric scrabbled at his eyelids, trying to scrape away the frost sealing them. A sea of white replaced the black, leaving his vision fuzzy. Jake had to get right in his face before the hazel eyes and green ski mask upgraded from multicolored blob status. Eric shook his head, clearing it enough to make out the finer details of the bleached trees stretching over their heads. He grunted before getting up, nose tingling with the scent of wintergreen from a dead branch on the ground.

"Yeah, just a bad dream is all. One *hell* of a bad dream."

Jake lifted himself half a foot higher with a meaty arm that looked shrink-wrapped into the sleeve of his parka. Brushing off the snow covering his body, he snapped a twig off the nearest limb and broke it in half.

"Too bad we can't wake up from this one, huh?"

Eric nodded, the warmth held in by the snow's insulation rapidly evaporating. He looked into the open backpack at his feet, the open cans of Miller gaping at him in silent laughter. His stomach growled while his gloved hands pawed through the contents.

Still empty. I guess running out of food wasn't just a nightmare, either.

Jake slapped him on the back. His friend's grunt escaped in a cloud.

"No offense, but the next time you wing a buck, just let the sucker go. No matter how big the antlers are."

Eric nodded, picking up his rifle from where he'd left it against the tree that had served as his backrest. The creature flashed through his mind, fur as white as the drifts. The rack on its head put the three trophies he'd already collected to shame.

That big bastard must have been twelve points easy. And he just kept teasing us.

He shivered, sucking in a breath of frozen air. Even

though the snowfall had lightened, the chill of the flash storm the day before felt like it was stuck in the marrow of his bones. Just the thought of walking in it made him feel off balance.

What the hell is wrong with you? You've been hunting damn near since you could walk, and you got your ass turned around like a proper chump by a little snow and some stupid deer.

Eric could still see the buck flitting through the gusts of snow like a ghost, taunting him.

Always at a bad angle or out of range. I was lucky I even nicked his hide. But God, I wanted him so bad.

He grimaced.

Or maybe it was just the beer.

The muscles in his abdomen clenched involuntarily, forcing out a gurgle. He looked down at his stomach.

Thank God we dressed warm enough to make it through the night, anyway. Next time, I just need to make sure to pack more food instead of booze. Two sandwiches definitely don't do it when the shit hits the fan.

Eric pulled on his pack and called to his friend.

"You ready?"

Jake nodded, shouldering his own load.

"Yeah, let's get cracking already. I don't have much interest in spending another night out here." He rapped the half of the twig in his hand against one of the tree trunks. "I don't know what it is about the trees out here, but they give me the creeps."

Eric grinned, walking up alongside him.

"You should be honored. I showed Dad a photo of the cabin when I bought it, but you're the first person

I've brought out here with me. Which probably makes you only the second person to see any of this in at least a hundred years. Maybe a couple hundred."

Jake ducked under the first few branches in their way.

"Ah, but we're the first people to get lost here together. That's what's important."

Eric tried to laugh, but the pain in his gut stifled it. Big man that he was, the lost calories were adding up quick. Visions of roast turkey and BBQ ribs were passing through his mind when he bumped into his friend.

"Ah, crap. Sorry, man."

Jake's voice came out as thin as the spindly branches he'd navigated.

"Uh, Eric. Didn't we break through a bunch of shit getting to that little spot we holed up in?"

"Yeah. And we're going to use it to backtrack now that we can actually see what we're doing. What about it?"

Jake cleared his throat.

"Do you . . . see any broken branches around here? Anywhere?"

Eric peered over his friend's head, scanning the area before aiming a double-take back the way they'd come.

"Uh . . . okay? What the fuck? Where the hell *did* we come in?"

Jake shook his head.

"I-I don't know, man. I really don't. What do you think we should do?"

Eric pushed his face deeper into his parka as a blast of wind peppered him with a fresh layer of snow. Even with just his eyes and mouth exposed, the cold seemed to seep inside him, adding a new layer of ice to what lingered from the day before. His limbs tightened while the sensation grew and spread. He could swear he felt it running through his veins and pumping right into his heart. The pain in his stomach swelled until Eric couldn't tell if it was hunger or nausea.

S-s-so . . . s—so . . .

Jake shook him, but the feeling stayed inside. Festering.

"Eric! Are you *sure* you're okay, man? You look like you're ready to have a heart attack or something."

Eric took several shallow breaths, trying to fight the sensation back. Steadying himself against one of the nearby trees, he caught his reflection in the layer of ice coating the trunk. The image was worse quality than a funhouse mirror, but there was no mistaking the light shining from his eyes. It intensified, transfixing him. Filling him even as his stomach constricted to his spine. He barely managed a whisper.

"It's funny. I think one of the dreams I had last night came true."

Jake smiled, a measure of relief in his voice at the words.

"Anything positive is welcome at this point. I hope it was a good one."

Eric's lips pulled back until they ached. The wind rose with his rasp, and when his eyes met Jake's, his friend's went wide. Eric shook his head.

"No, it was something bad."

His hand reached for the hunting knife sheathed over the small of his back.

"Something hungry."

CHAPTER 1

EMMA RAWLINS LEANED back and watched a blade longer than her body flash across the screen. A gout of blood the tint of cherry Kool-Aid splashed the wall behind the victim. The final girl's best friend went down clutching her throat. A chortle shot through Emma's straw, the bubbling of her root beer dubbing what should have been a death rattle.

"Shh!"

Emma glanced around, ready to lob a handful of popcorn. The theater was too dark to identify the proper target. She spoke just loud enough to be heard over the score.

"Bite me."

Attention back on the screen, the movie finally earned its one and only shudder. There was a close-up of the victim's eyes. They stared through Emma, vacant . . . pleading. A sudden mist drifted into her mind, distorting the image into one far more familiar. Her fingers clutched the armrest as she leaned forward, whispering an apology she'd never gotten to make.

"Mom, I . . . "

The effect only lasted until the camera panned back

far enough to show off the seeping neck wound the special effects department must have worked so hard on. The blood cleansed Emma's vision, but her sense of fun had already been washed away. The gore had somehow gone from over-the-top amusement to insulting, and no amount of junk food could get rid of the bad taste coating her tongue.

Man, they really got the color wrong . . .

CHAPTER 2

EMMA KNEW SHE was screwed before she could even flip the light switch. An exhale nearby destroyed the silence she'd hoped to maintain. The stink of tobacco drifted into her nose and dragged a cough from her lungs.

"It's an hour past your curfew, young lady."

Emma rolled her eyes before flicking the switch. Her father watched her from his seat at the kitchen table, the brown eyes inscrutable behind the lenses of his glasses. Smoke drifted up from the Marlboro smoking in his hand.

Emma dug in her jacket pocket for her phone before holding it out.

"My cell died. The stupid alarm never went off."

"Try again, kiddo."

Emma fought to maintain eye contact with her father. Her finger pressed on the cell's POWER button, the nail tapping on the dead screen a moment later.

"See?"

Her father stood, his thin, six-foot frame dwarfing Emma as he approached her and took the device from her hand. She hoped he didn't see her gorge rise and fall during the appraisal.

Buy it. You don't need to know I never went to Tina's. You don't need to know I snuck out to the movie you've been calling "filth" for the last two weeks and nobody has online. Just this once. Please, please buy it.

Emma's father glanced from the screen to her face. He pursed his lips, stretching the thick, black moustache.

"Oh, it's definitely dead. And so are your plans this weekend."

Emma's mouth fell open.

"But . . . but that's not fair! I didn't *do* anything!"

Her father's voice hit a colder note.

"You lied to my face." He handed her the phone. "I figured I'd call the theater when you were late. I asked the manager if your friend Tara was on duty tonight. You know, the one who's old enough to sneak 16-year-old girls into R-rated movies?" Her father paced in front of her, stroking his chin. "It's funny. I asked him to send one of the ushers to take a look around, and there was a girl who looked *exactly* like you walking out during the end credits." He stopped and swept a finger from Emma's feet to the collar of her jacket. "She even had the same outfit on and everything. Crazy, huh?" His eyes narrowed.

Crap! Think of something, think of something . . .

Her father sighed and removed his glasses. Emma cringed at the prominent eye sockets that had been hiding behind the lenses. Lately, the skin seemed to stretch just a little tighter every time they were exposed.

"Daddy, you really should . . . "

Her father wiped the lenses with his sleeve.

"You're grounded. Two weeks. Considering that's how long I told you 'no,' it seems appropriate."

Heat rose in Emma's cheeks, but she couldn't help chuckling as she glared at him.

"'Grounded?' From *what?* I'm not allowed to *do* anything! No dating, no pets, no R-rated movies. God, Dad, aside from chores and school, you've barely even let me leave the house since—"

"That's *enough!*" Her father's finger trembled in her face. "That's enough." His voice lowered, becoming gentle. "Honey, I know things have been tough on you this year, but it's for a good reason."

Emma exhaled, blowing a strand of dyed blonde hair into the smoke.

"Sure, Dad. Let's be scared forever. Let's live in a vault." She shook her head and headed for the stairs. "Don't worry about sending me to my room. I'm going to bed."

Emma felt more tired with each step, the weight that had been building up for months all but dragging her onto her mattress. She looked on the night through the shatter-proof windowpane, her nose twitching at the mélange of gun oil and food waiting to be pressure-sealed. The scent wafted to her from her father's workroom across the hall, making her almost hungry enough to go back downstairs after the empty calories of a popcorn dinner. Emma turned over and buried her nose in a pillow—tried to remember how cool air felt blowing into her room. Her mother's touch.

She pulled the sheets over her head when she noticed there was just light enough to illuminate the bug-out bag lying bloated against the closet door beside her backpack.

A week of supplies, just like you insisted, Dad. She pushed her face harder into the pillow. *Never mind we're talking about a week after an emergency that's never going to happen.*

Visions of blood and shattered glass played behind Emma's eyelids while she tried to sleep. Her hand tried to wipe away drops of cold rain that weren't there. And she heard her father's every footstep as he made his way upstairs and closed the door to his workroom behind him, readying more food, more guns, more ammo. She heard him humming a Rolling Stones song when the evening's first magazine snapped into place.

So many bullets. And for what? For what? Another burglar? An army?

Emma squeezed her eyes shut until they ached, but the noises filled her head where there should have been night sounds through an open window. Still, she knew from past arguments that the songs of the outside world came at too high a price.

CHAPTER 3

EMMA STOOD OUTSIDE the movie theater. *Instead of the light snow that had settled on her shoulders that night, torrents of rain ate through her jacket and soaked her skin. She ran under the outcropping. To the doors.*

She shivered as she wrenched at the handle, a gust of cold air freezing the water to her flesh. The doors trembled, but refused to budge.

Open, damn it!

It was only then she realized how dark it was inside. The area holding the concession stand was pitch black. The ticket booth, empty. She pounded on the glass.

"Tara! Are you in there? Let me in!"

Emma jumped back when four rows of tiny bulbs flared to life on the lobby wall. She squinted, distance making the image at the center of the lights indistinct while her eyes struggled to adjust. When they did, she backed away until her heels struck the curb, the downpour drenching her.

W-what . . . ?

Emma stared into her mother's eye sockets, her open mouth just visible above the bottom border of the poster's frame. Tendrils of darkness poked from the three voids like tiny worms, swarming over the bulbs and squirming toward the floor.

Toward her.

"No . . . no! No!"

Emma turned to flee when the first strand of black slipped under the doors and wrapped around her ankle. The dark thread squelched against her flesh, spreading out from the pressure of its own grip before it pulled. She fell hard, her side striking concrete. When she opened her mouth to scream, the darkness rushed in, sliding between her teeth and covering her tongue in a foul oil slick. Free of the ooze, the lights glared at her around her mother's face while Emma mimicked her death mask. The blackness thickened in her throat, pushing from the inside until she heard a snap.

Emma woke up. She was retching phantom liquid out of her lungs when she saw the dark figure leaning over her. This time, she could scream. The shape recoiled as her fingernails slashed for its black hole of a face. Her father's voice grunted when one of the points struck home.

"Emma! What's the matter with you?"

She rubbed her eyes, the light filtering in from the open door finally bringing her father's features into focus.

"Dad?" Emma glanced at her bedside alarm clock. "It's two in the morning. What—"

Her father pushed her bag into her hand. "No time."

His gaze flitted around the room. "You have everything ready like I showed you, right?" He shook the bag. "Your gear?"

Another drill. Seriously? We just had one last week.

Emma was mid-groan when she saw the frantic light in her father's eyes. She didn't have long to look before he was pulling her off the bed.

"Come on! I've got everything loaded up in the car."

Emma yanked the bag out of his grip.

"What are you talking about? I'm not even dressed!" She threw the bag down. "Dad! You're freaking out! You're freaking *me* out! What's going on? *Tell me!*"

"Stop arguing and get in the *damn car!*"

Emma stood as tall as her 5-feet-3 inches would allow and crossed her arms.

"No. Not until you *talk* to me."

Emma's father lifted his glasses and rubbed his eyes with a shaking hand. Without warning, he wrapped her in a hug. His hold was so tight, she barely registered the sting in her arm.

"Dad . . . ?"

Emma's legs went weak. She slid to the floor, held up only by her father's embrace. The panic from her dream dug a fresh set of claws in her mind when he began to blur with the rest of the room, and darkness swallowed him with everything else.

His voice barely registered in her ears, but she could still make out the pain in its tone. "I'm sorry, honey. I'm so sorry. But we really have to go . . . "

CHAPTER 4

EMMA BARELY FOUND the strength to open her eyes when she came to. Her body felt heavy, as if her insides had been replaced with lead. It took several long minutes before the movement of the car and the texture of the upholstery penetrated the fog in her head. So did the sharp hiss of her father's breath as he made a hard turn on the road.

I . . . wh-where . . . ?

Her father took a quick look at her over his shoulder. Some of the intensity in his eyes had faded. But not nearly enough.

"Try to lay still. It's going to be a little while before that sedative finishes working its way out of your system."

Emma tried to sit up, but a wave of nausea and lightheadedness overpowered her before she'd gone up an inch. A grimace twisted her expression.

Her father sighed. "Why don't you ever listen to me?"

He shifted in his seat. "Then again, I suppose you don't have much choice right now."

He cleared his throat, and Emma didn't have to see him wet his lips to know what was coming.

A . . . speech? Now?

"You said you wanted to know what was going on, right? Well, I'll tell you. It's the end. Of everything." The hairs of his moustache rustled under his fingers. "The network I'm plugged into has seen it coming for months now. Years, really. All the indicators are lit up like Christmas lights." Her father lifted a hand and ticked each point off on his digits. "Volcanic activity, seismic activity, socio-economic factors: they're all there." He stabbed the wheel with his index finger, as if adding ending punctuation to his argument.

The car buckled back and forth as it hit rough road. Emma's body pushed deeper into the back of her seat while the vehicle climbed.

"The end of civilization is going to be a messy business. *Very* messy. Some people will step on anyone to get what they want. Certain . . . people have even been waiting for it. When the guillotine falls, there's going to be chaos. And it's only going to spread."

Emma twitched her fingers, her nerves coming back to her control. She could almost lift herself by the time the car stopped. Her father exited and opened her car door, reaching out to her. A log cabin stood behind him half the size of their modest home. His lips spread in a pinched smile.

"Fortunately for us, we'll be nowhere near it."

CHAPTER 5

EMMA SLID PAST her father's hand and out of the car. Just trying to bear her own weight made her dizzy, and she had to place a palm atop the car's roof for support. She looked upon the cabin, the snow-covered trees poking from the ground like the skeletal hands of a giant—anywhere but at her father.

I . . . I kept hoping he'd get better. But it's never going to happen. Ever. He's lost it. He's lost . . .

Tears welled in her eyes when she tried to reconcile the gentle parent of her youth—the man who read her bedtime stories, built her treehouse, and scared away the monsters under her bed—with someone willing to pump her full of drugs to avoid an argument.

Just because it was faster! Faster!

Emma wiped at the tears threatening to fall.

Jesus Christ . . . who are you?

The hand that fell atop Emma's head, trying to stroke her hair, felt like talons. She and her father pulled away from each other at the same instant. Still unsteady, Emma lost her balance and crashed ass-first into four inches of snow. She scrambled backward in an awkward crabwalk when her father knelt to help her up. He lifted his hands, the palms turning red from cold.

"Em . . . Emmie . . . it's okay."

"The hell it is!" She rolled up the sleeve of the jacket that had been put on her, prodding the little wound the needle had left behind. "Does *this* look okay to you? *Really?"*

Her father hung his head before giving a slight nod.

"You're right. I'm sorry. But I didn't have time to convince you. To argue with you." He stood up, dusting off the snow clinging to his pants. "And I'd much rather have you mad at me than dead."

Emma staggered up, trying to dry her freezing fingers on the front of her jacket.

"Because it's the end of the world? Do you really not understand how crazy that sounds?" She looked him in the eye, all the resentment of the last year finally boiling out of her. "Everything we've done since Mom died was crazy."

Her father slammed the car door before wagging a finger at her.

"Don't you bring her into this! If I'd been smarter then . . . " He shook his head. "Please, you're cold. I'm cold. Let's at least get inside and warm up. We can talk there."

Emma was ready to refuse before she noticed the numbness creeping through her legs. Even the bit of forearm poking from her sleeve was covered in gooseflesh.

"Fine."

Her father walked to the back of the car and popped the trunk. He had two massive bags slung over each shoulder before he led the way to the front door. Even through the canvas, Emma caught the familiar tang of gun oil. Muttering, he juggled the bags and hunted in the front pocket of his shirt until he extracted a key.

Emma didn't know what to expect when the door swung open. Part of her had been bracing for animal heads on the walls and a swarm of bugs to flee the light spilling across the floor. A hillbilly's lair. Instead, the place was stripped down to essentials and cleaned almost to the point of being antiseptic. Every piece of furniture inside from the living room couch to the bookcases was new and feng shuied.

Emma sniggered at her reflection in the polished floorboards and the stairs leading to the next floor.

I guess even Dad's inner caveman has OCD.

She flinched when her father pointed a finger over her shoulder.

"Your room is down the hall past the living room. First door on the right. You go ahead and take a load off while I get your things."

Doing as she was told, Emma heard her father grumble as the bags jostled against each other, canvas rustling while he climbed the stairs.

Get out . . . I've got to get out of here!

Her hand immediately went to the pocket that had held her cell phone, only to find it empty. She didn't recall seeing any phones in the rooms she'd passed by, either.

Shit! Fuck! Of course he made sure I couldn't get a hold of anyone. She swatted at the flakes still clinging to her clothes. *And there's zero chance I'd make it more than a mile or two in that weather.*

Pausing in her room's doorway, her ears picked up the jingling of keys overhead before a door clicked shut.

At least now I know where he keeps the guns. So much for making him drive us home.

Despite all he'd done, Emma felt bile rise at the thought of pointing a weapon at her father.

Even if I got that far, I'd never be able to pull the trigger. I'll bet he knows it, too.

She began to sit on the bed before the water squelching in her pants convinced her to wait for her bag. It gave her a few minutes to take in the Spartan décor surrounding her. A bookcase with a few choice volumes of crazy on the shelves, a squat twin bed with a camo blanket, and a window on the wall. A steel shutter was suspended over it in place of drapes.

Probably safety glass, too. Just like home. Great.

Emma looked outside at the forest of naked trees. Even the bark clear of the snow was white. She watched the wind blow the drifts between the trunks, the flakes swirling toward the cabin in visible gusts. The wind gained strength, blowing the snow and spinning higher into the air, the cloud thickening in spots as it pulled fresh powder from the ground. A rapid succession of Rorschach images blew across the landscape.

For just a second, one almost looked like an open mouth.

Emma blinked, the impression already gone by the time she opened her eyes. She tweaked her forehead.

God, get a grip, girl. You've got bigger problems than snow.

A knock on the door drew her attention from the scene outside.

"Em?"

"Just leave it out there." She held her head in her hands. "Just leave it."

Emma waited until her father's footsteps had faded out of earshot before cracking the door wide enough to pull her bug-out bag inside. She opened it up, pulling out a fresh pair of pants and underwear when she caught the window in her peripheral vision. Glancing back and forth between the clothes and the thick flakes striking the pane, she bit her lip and pulled the shutter down.

CHAPTER 6

"Em! TIME FOR DINNER!"

From atop the bed, Emma looked over her knees to the door. Her will fought what felt to be a nest of rats chewing at her insides, but the growl that bubbled from her guts spoke of larger creatures.

"I'm not hungry."

Past the door, her father sighed.

"Now, I know that's not true. We were on the road for—"

Emma leaned forward. "How long?"

Searching the room, she realized she'd been too absorbed in the insanity of the situation to look for a clock. "Dad?"

A tiny vibration trembled through the door as her father either leaned against it or rested his hand against the wood.

"It was a long trip, honey."

"How long?"

Emma imagined her father fussing with his moustache.

"Seventeen hours."

"Seventeen *hours?*" Emma was off the bed and pacing to the door. Her hand was nearly on the knob before she relented. Images of her friends' faces, her town, flitted across her mind like photographs. Their presence felt every bit as distant.

Jesus . . . I was out for that long?

She rubbed her arm.

And the dose of whatever he gave me was that exact?

The next question slipped out of her mouth, but it was directed at herself rather than her father.

"Where the hell are we?"

The feet beyond the door scuffed. "Wisconsin."

Emma blinked, trying to conjure the state's position in her head. While the U.S. map in her brain was fuzzy, the length of the mental line cutting from point to point was accurate enough to frighten her. She finally opened the door, looking up at her father and hoping she was wrong.

"But that's . . . halfway across the country, isn't it?"

Her father closed his eyes. His fingers massaged the bridge of his nose, making his glasses jump when he nodded.

Emma stared at him, the shapes of states she'd never even stepped foot in flashing past her eyes.

Of course. It was seventeen fucking hours. Where else would we have ended up?

She fought the ache in her head, her heart, and tried to find the old familiarity in her father's face. Emma pleaded with it while she rubbed her wrist, remembering how her motherss had slowed until it disappeared.

"Daddy . . . I want to go home."

He tried to smile, but something about the way his lips stretched distorted the presentation into a wince.

Her father bent, placing a hand on each of her shoulders.

"Em, I know it's hard to accept, but this *is* home now. We just have to make the best of it."

Emma broke eye contact and looked down at her shoes. Through the shutter, Emma heard the wind whistle past the window. She didn't know if the chill worming through her came from the sound or her father's touch.

"You said to come in and warm up earlier. I don't think that's going to happen."

Her father's hand slipped off her and back to his side. An unpleasant tingle stayed behind.

"It's a big adjustment. I understand that. Really. But this place will grow on you if you give it some time."

Emma cursed the growl rising in her stomach. This time, her father did manage a smile.

"Meanwhile, why don't we put that beast to bed? It'll give us a chance to talk."

Don't you mean, "listen?"

Still, the hunger decided her. The ache inside was becoming a full-on cramp. She followed her father down the hall and around the corner into a fully stocked kitchen. Cans and canisters with handwritten labels lined shelves from floor to ceiling. The sink was retro, but the stove looked more advanced than the one in their house. One burner glowed red-hot while something bubbled in a pot atop the range. The smell of fresh chili got Emma's mouth watering.

Ugh . . . why does he have to be such a good cook?

Emma slid into a chair, allowing her father to fill the bowl in front of her. She didn't bother blowing on it, letting the liquid scald her tongue on the way in. The bowl was half-empty by the time her father spoke, the half-smile on his face spreading wider.

"Not so bad, huh?"

He hummed a few notes before popping a spoonful of chili into his mouth. Emma's chewing slowed while he continued, smacking his lips between bites.

"We're totally self-sufficient here. Off the grid. About the only real problem is keeping the pipes from freezing. You wouldn't believe how much insul—"

"Stop it." The chili went down Emma's throat like battery acid. "Just. Stop."

"Stop what?"

Emma swirled the spoon in her bowl. "Pretending like we're on vacation. Some family trip. You kidnapped me. Drugged me! And took me how many hundreds of miles away from my friends, our house . . . " She shook her head. "Everything."

Her father shifted in his chair. "Only because—"

"I know! I know . . . what you said in the car. The end of the world, socio-economic . . . something! But where's all this awful stuff we're running from? Where's the *proof*?"

Her father took off his glasses, folding them and placing them neatly on the table.

"Honey, Rome wasn't built in a day, but it damn near fell in one." He stared into his bowl, the lines near his eyes deepening. "This country isn't any better. Debt, inflation, militarized police, wars that never really end . . . we've been circling the toilet for a long time. We're just . . . *due*." He lifted his haunted gaze to her own. "I managed to get us out days—maybe hours—before the whole world came down on our heads. Isn't that better than fighting tooth and nail through a mob of crazy people?"

Emma abandoned the spoon, her hand balling into a fist.

"So how long do we wait, then? A month? A year? How long would it take for you to realize those guys you talk to are full of shit?"

Her father raised his finger at her. "Don't—"

"What, Dad? Call them out on it after all . . . this?" Her fingernails bit deeper into her palm. "What else did you expect me to do?"

Her father pushed his own bowl of chili away, a disgusted look on his face. He rested his chin on his hand when he looked back at her, frustration in his eyes.

"What would it take, Em? To make you understand? To *work* with me a little?"

Emma noticed a clock affixed to the wall, the second hand ticking down.

"I want a time limit. And not a crazy one, either. If we make it through that and nothing happens, I want your word we'll go back home and you'll never do something like this to me again."

Her father glared at her, his lips going thin. "Six months."

"One."

"Four. My final offer."

The faces of her friends—her life—retreated down a long, dark tunnel.

But it'll still be there. Waiting for me . . . right? She bit her lip. *And I bet I could get hold of the car keys in just a few weeks if I'm careful enough.* Her foot twitched against the leg of her chair. *God, I can't believe I'm doing this . . .*

Emma met his gaze, flinching only when a blast of frigid air dragged a chorus of creaks from the roof. She fancied she could feel the cold settling in her bones.

"Deal."

CHAPTER 7

EMMA PACED HER ROOM.

If I can't figure something out and get away with it, I've got four months . . . four fucking months . . .

Looking around, she realized she didn't even have a calendar to mark the days. Instead, the paranoid titles of her father's books whispered to her about the hours yet to pass. She kicked the bug-out bag to the corner. Frustration staunched the welling tears before they could drip to the floor.

No phone, no computer, no movies. Not even a poster, for Christ's sake!

The window rattled behind the metal barrier. Echoes of a high-pitched gust tingled in Emma's ears, raising the fine hairs on her arms. She rubbed the limbs, trying to subdue the sudden outbreak of gooseflesh until the noise passed.

Damn, Dad. I really wish you would've at least let me grab my iPod.

Shivering, Emma snatched the blanket off the bed and wrapped it around herself like a cloak. She scowled, drawing deeper into it.

And it's fucking freezing on top of it. Location,

location, location, Dad. Just like Mom used to say when she was selling a house.

She dropped onto the bed and let her weight carry her side to the mattress.

God, I wonder what she would've said about all this . . .

Emma shook her head, trying to banish the image of her mother's face before it could materialize in her mind. The smiles, the warmth of her hands. The blood dripping from her mouth.

She slapped her cheek.

"Enough of that crap."

Reaching over, Emma slid one of the books off the case. Flipping to page one, she dog-eared the corner.

One down, about a hundred and nineteen to go.

Returning the book to its place, she pulled the blanket over her head and wadded the fabric against her ears. The wind roared on, barely muffled. The sound felt like it was creeping in through the cracks along with the winter air, infecting the room with its cadence. Its coldness. Both trickled inside Emma, making her bite her lip until she clawed back to the light. Panting, she bathed in the glow of the lamp, remembering the weight of the book in her hands. The waiting pages. The waiting days. She rubbed the spots from her eyes before she set her head back on the pillow, the hours sedated in the car's backseat making the lids difficult to close.

I wonder if I can steal the car ahead of schedule . . .

Emma rolled out of her bed and into the snow.

Sputtering, she spat the flakes from her mouth and swatted the glittering white off her night clothes. The flecks glinted in the sparse moonlight streaming through the clouds overhead. She groped for the bed behind her only to find empty air. Whirling around, there was no sign of the cabin—only trees transformed into puppets by the force of the wind bending their branches.

"D-Dad!" *Emma held herself, willing her teeth to stop chattering, before taking a tentative step toward where she thought the cabin was supposed to be.* "Dad! Are you there?"

The darkness around her deepened as if in answer, the clouds above thickening until the full moon held no more power than a child's dying nightlight. The cold intensified, too, spreading numbness from Emma's toes up through her shins. She trudged on with both legs all but dead, her knees sinking in the drifts.

"Dad! Please! Where are you?"

The night pressed tighter with each step, poised to snap her up, when a light flickered through the blizzard.

God . . . oh, thank God . . .

Emma rushed toward the glow as best she could, the outline of the cabin gradually penetrating the haze. A flame danced behind a window on the ground floor, and as she got closer, she saw her father's silhouette watching her through the glass.

"Daddy!"

Emma's hand was poised to bang on the windowpane when her palm froze in midair. The candle in her father's hand flickered, dimly illuminating the room around him, but the hand holding it was as black as the night outside. Featureless, her father's silhouette stooped and cocked its head. The breath was still escaping her throat when the shadow slammed its face through the glass and melted into hers.

Emma woke with a gasp, kicking her way backward until her spine hit the headboard. She pulled the blanket around her more tightly when she caught the shadow shifting on the wall, only gradually recognizing its movements as reflections of her own. Trembling, she took a deep breath and tottered toward her double, her lungs aching until her hand crushed the five black fingers. Despite the cold sweat clinging to her body, Emma's cheeks began to burn.

God, girl. Night terrors. Scared of your own shadow. Just how old are you, anyway?

She tapped a finger on the wall, giggling at the absurdity of the situation until the unfamiliar texture stifled her amusement. The wind groaned outside, probing just far enough through the window to coax a shiver. Emma closed her eyes.

I guess this mess being a dream would be way too much to hope for.

Too awake to lie back down, Emma lifted the shutter and watched the snow whip past the pane. The trees were indistinct, their spindly boughs intertwining as if they were holding onto one another for mutual support against the onslaught. The longer Emma looked, the more the wood blurred into a wall, giving new texture to the darkness. It rippled like black velvet with each gust, a swelling tidal wave. Emma slammed the shutter back down with a fresh layer of ice water on her face.

CHAPTER 8

HOW'D YOU SLEEP?"

Emma watched her father's hopeful smile wilt under a well-aimed glare. Clearing his throat, he turned his attention back to the eggs cooking on the stove.

Emma took a sip from the cup of coffee waiting for her on the table. Her mouth puckered at the drink's bitterness, but she ignored the sugar and creamer at her elbow.

"That stupid wind kept me up all night."

Her father reached for the bag of bread on the counter and pushed two slices into the toaster. "Winters around here are usually pretty harsh. It should start calming down in a couple months, though."

Emma rubbed her eyes and took a long draught of her coffee.

Great.

The eggs sizzled while she again took stock of the kitchen. While it had fewer rooms, each part of the cabin appeared larger than its counterpart back home, making her feel even shorter than usual. Every cabinet seemed out of reach.

"Where did you find this place, anyway?"

Her father scraped the eggs off the skillet with a spatula before depositing them on a plate.

"It belonged to a friend of mine. Or his son, actually. He was a big outdoorsman. Practically lived out here himself. Poor kid was only about thirty when he had an accident. His dad just wanted to get rid of the thing when it passed to him. Too many memories, I guess. He was selling it for a song, so I snapped it up." He carried the plate of scrambled eggs over and set it on the table. "You want ketchup?"

Emma took another sip of her coffee before shaking her head. She stabbed a forkful, debating whether the eggs would play nice with the dirt aftertaste stuck to her palate.

"So, what kind of accident was it?"

Her father shrugged before going to collect the toast. "Disappeared with a friend of his out here about the same time a blizzard rolled through. The storm must've caught them out hunting. They never found any bodies—just the truck. The kid's dad was still pretty broken up about it. I can't say I blame him." His fingers hovered over the toast before pulling it out. "Losing someone . . . like that. I can't even imagine. I really can't."

The flash of sadness Emma saw in her father's eyes stung. It wasn't hard for her to remember when she saw it all the time. Both on his face and in the mirror.

You know you can. But who would want to?

Emma took a bite of the eggs. Tabasco sauce and cheddar cheese played on her tongue along with the salt and pepper.

Just the way I like it.

A tiny shred of guilt picked at her.

Damn it, Dad. Of all the weird hobbies, why did you have to buy into one that made you act so . . . so nuts?

She chewed another mouthful, already knowing the answer as she watched her father flit back and forth in front of the stove.

It's always been about fear, hasn't it? I'm really the last thing left you give a damn about, aren't I? The last part of Mom you can protect. The last part of her that someone can take away.

Emma barely got the eggs down. She wanted to hug her father and scream at him at the same time. To make him understand what he refused to see. But as always, she couldn't find the words.

Her father returned to the table, the butter knife in his hand smearing strawberry jam across the toast. His first piece disappeared in three large bites. He nodded toward the kitchen window.

"I'll show you around after breakfast. It's beautiful out here. No pollution, no noise, no traffic . . . "

Emma downed the rest of her coffee.

No people, either. I guess bears are more trustworthy.

She speared another piece of egg, muttering.

"Hibernation would be great about now."

"What?"

"Nothing," Emma said, lifting her fork to her mouth. "Just talking to myself."

Her father's eyebrow raised while she chewed, staying up until he shrugged and bit into the other piece of toast on his plate. The rest of the meal passed in silence. When it was over, he took the dirty dishes and deposited them in the sink before walking to the closet. He came back with a green parka in one hand and a hat and gloves in the other. A pair of long johns was draped over his shoulder.

Emma stared at the ugly things until her father chuckled.

"I know they're not much for looks, but they'll keep your legs warm. Now, go get changed. We've got work to do."

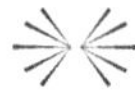

Emma followed her father through the snow, the barrel of the rifle slung over his shoulder glaring light into her eyes. She winced and fought the urge to scratch at the itch prickling her thighs. The parka was so thick, she doubted she'd even be able to reach.

Cripes, I feel like that little kid in A Christmas Story.

She caught up to her father as he stopped at the tree line, examining the lower branches.

"What do you see, Em?"

She glanced at the snapped ends of the twigs near her father's pointing finger. "From the height, it looks like a coyote or fox went through. Maybe a bobcat. Tough to tell for sure with no hairs and the prints filled in."

"Good girl."

"Kind of hard to forget when you made me read that book on tracking three times over." She rolled her eyes. "And tested me on it."

He laughed.

"Well, it stuck, didn't it?"

Emma yawned and looked out at the expanse of wilderness before them. Beyond the clearing where the cabin stood, the forest seemed to stretch on forever. The swaying of the tree limbs gave her uncomfortable flashbacks of her dream.

"Just how much of this are we going to check, anyway? Our nearest neighbors are probably in the next state."

Her father readjusted the rifle's strap.

"I doubt we'll have any trouble for a while yet out here, if at all, but that's no excuse to be lazy. Securing the perimeter is important, and it's a job I want you to take seriously."

Emma grumbled and followed him past a half-mile tangle of trees before they hit a rise and turned, slowly carving a large square around the cabin as they went. There was nothing to find but white and the skeletons of the trees. She was huffing by the time they made it back to the front door, her nose threatening to spill snot that would only freeze to her lip. She glanced at the car, its gleaming red metal largely clear of the snow covering everything else.

He must've cleaned it off this morning.

She bit her lip, eyeing the steering wheel while her father dusted the flakes from his hat. A puff of crystallized air escaped her mouth.

I don't even know where he keeps the keys. She looked at the growing layer of white surrounding it in disgust. *Not that I'd be able to get any traction in this mess. Unless I get lucky . . .*

She looked up when the front door creaked open to find her father at the threshold, holding the door open for her.

"Coming, coming," she muttered, jogging for the steps. Her father caught her by the arm before she could make it past him. He wore the same expression as the night he'd caught her sneaking back in.

Shit.

Emma put on her best innocent-little-girl face—the one that reduced most of her groundings to slaps on the wrist.

"Daddy?"

She watched his face twitch in the direction of the car for just a moment before he released her. He sighed.

"Nothing," he said. A smile flitted across his lips. "It's nothing. Get inside. I'll make us some hot chocolate."

Emma wiped the flecks of ice from her cheek only for the wind to blast her back with a fresh torrent of powder. She tried to sputter a curse around the strands of hair that had blown into her mouth and failed. Slamming the door, she pulled off her parka and stomped through the specks of white littering the floor. Her father called to her as he placed a kettle under the head of the faucet.

"Don't get too comfortable. There's still lots to do today."

With my luck, it's probably latrine duty.

A hiss escaped the faucet when her father turned the handle, but no water came out. He placed the kettle in the sink and turned the handle as far as it would go. Then the other. The effort didn't earn a drop. Emma stopped en route to the table when the faucet's protests finally died with a gurgle.

"I'm guessing that's a rain check on the hot chocolate?"

Her father stooped slightly before readjusting the handles.

"The pipes just froze, that's all. It's nothing serious, but we do need to take care of it before it gets any worse. Come on."

Emma followed him to the living room. Moving the coffee table aside and lifting the rug, her father pulled a key from his pants pocket. A click came when it fitted into a crack in the floor. He gave a hard yank, lifting a square section free of the boards, several inches of steel gleaming under the wood. A light flickered to life in the darkness below.

Emma looked from her father to the pit and back again. She was still processing the trapdoor when her father's foot reached the halfway point down the stairs. He glanced back at her.

"Em? Are you coming?"

She squinted at the dimly lit space below. Everything under her looked like it was carved out of concrete, and a faint, moldy smell drifted to her nose that made her think of open graves. She grimaced and placed her foot on the first step.

I sure wish I didn't have to.

Reaching the bottom, an overflow from the kitchen waited for her. Half the area was crammed from floor to ceiling with enough preserved goods to fill a corner store. The other side held an assortment of tools. Crisscrossed between the two, a network of pipes loomed in the air, the metal obscured under thick layers of insulation. Emma balked at the reality of what she was seeing.

This isn't just a basement. It's a safe room. Hell, a bomb shelter!

Her father pulled a stepladder from the corner and set to prying at the nearest piece of the stuff. It crunched in his hands, barely able to peel away even when the veins in his forehead stood out. Several quick bursts of crystallized air escaped his mouth before he threw the insulation to the ground. He pointed at the same corner he'd gone to for the ladder.

"Em, get that torch down there, would you? And those gloves and goggles, too."

Torch?

Searching, she found a tool with a small gas canister attached. Two heavy gloves were wrapped around it, held in place by the goggles' strap. Carrying the lot to her father, he plucked them from her fingers and set the goggles over his glasses. He tucked the torch under his arm while he slipped on the gloves.

"Thanks, honey. Now, stand clear."

Stepping back, Emma heard several clicks while she watched him toy with the torch. Then, a blue flame burst to life at the end of the nozzle. Her father lifted it near the pipe, keeping it just out of reach of the metal.

"It really wasn't supposed to be this cold yet. It doesn't take too long for pipes to start freezing over in these conditions. A few more hours like this and one of the things might have burst. We'll have to crank the heat up for a while and leave the faucet dripping."

Emma watched the flame go out while her father descended and moved the stepladder to the next length of pipe.

"Wouldn't that mean we'd have no water?"

"No *running* water," he said, climbing up. "We'd still have plenty in bottles."

Oh, so just no showers or working toilets. That's just fine, then. Awesome.

Her father grunted as he tore the next layer of insulation free. Emma shielded her eyes when the torch's flame burst to life again. The process continued in the same way until they reached the last section. This time, her father descended and stood atop the insulation, pulling the gloves and goggles off. He handed them to Emma

"This one's yours. You saw how I turned the torch on, yeah?"

"Yeah."

"Good. Just be careful."

Emma put on the safety equipment and climbed, taking the torch from her father before starting it up. She kept the flame just shy of the metal, just as he had shown her. Being above him, working, unsettled her.

It's not like you to trust me with something like this without any practice. Are you trying to bond with me? Or just trying to distract me from the shitty situation you put us in?

She narrowed her eyes against the glare.

And who really *designed this part of the cabin? That trapdoor?* Her teeth clenched until her jaw ached. *Hell, does that "friend" you mentioned and his kid even exist at all? Or did you have this place made all on your own even when that pile of bills kept growing on your desk back home? When you only went in to see patients two or three times a month?*

The questions echoed even after she finished and all the fresh insulation was wrapped around the pipes, the old stuff hung to dry out in front of the fireplace upstairs. Emma listened to drops of water strike the row of buckets below the stuff, the noise making her long for a light summer rain instead of the endless snow.

"You okay, kiddo?"

Emma turned and looked into her father's face. The harder she looked, the easier it was to see the mask he was wearing. Hiding behind.

Or is that his real face now?

"My stomach hurts. Can I go lie down for a while?"

The flicker of concern—real concern—that flashed through his eyes almost made her feel better.

"Sure. Just let me know if you need anything. I'll leave your dinner in the fridge, okay?"

"Yeah. Sure."

Emma stalked to her room, a very real pain in her gut. She kept listening, hoping, but the wind still howled past the window, skimming the drifts. And no matter how hard Emma tried, every storm she imagined flooded her mind with white.

CHAPTER 9

EMMA WOKE TO WIND

The whistle filled her ears, flooding her skull until her brain threatened to freeze solid. She tried to block the sound, but her hands rose in fitful spasms from where they were buried in the snow. They numbed to rigidity before they could go higher than her chest.

"H-h-he . . ."

The word stalled on Emma's tongue, garbled by the clicking of her teeth. Every muscle in her body clenched, tightening harder while the gusts picked up. Her eyes closed under the blasts of frigid air, ice forming on the lids while the ebb and flow of the gales gave way to one massive roar.

The sound hit Emma like a brick wall, rattling her bones. The sinews in her legs stretched as the force snatched her from the snow, wrenching hard enough to drag out a scream when her knees popped free of their sockets.

"God!"

She pried her eyes open just wide enough to see the landscape thirty feet below her, the smoke from the cabin's chimney wafting past her face. She coughed on the familiar reek of her father's cigarettes.

Although the cold deepened, the wind no longer touched her; it merely carried her aloft. Floating in the eye of a hurricane, she watched the trees guarding the perimeter dance madly through the haze, different shades of the same white noise. The longer Emma watched, the more the two merged, dragging the rest of the landscape with it. The cabin soon disappeared, too—swallowed whole.

Still staring, Emma finally caught sight of her hands. Marble-white, they shimmered in the void, flickering, crumbling, until they dissolved altogether. The sensation plucked at the rest of her, pulling until all her parts scattered in a thousand directions.

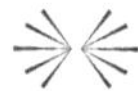

"Jesus!"

Emma tried to sit up and gasped at the pain shooting through her spine. Her bed loomed above her, the camo blanket dangling off the mattress and twisting around her legs.

"Fuck. *Me!*"

Emma thrashed until cool air played across the sweat coating her legs. She rubbed at her arms, flexing her fingers and savoring the color in her hands. Their heat.

No more. No more of this shit. No way. I'm done.

Emma got up and lifted the steel shutter just high enough to peek out her window. The snowfall had lightened, but the ground was still covered, any sign of whatever passed for a road still completely obscured.

But the car has four-wheel drive. Maybe it could get going if I dig it out a little and take it slow enough. Maybe . . .

Emma shook her head, trying to remember the last time she'd seen the keys.

That was when we came in the first day. Dad was still holding them when he brought that stuff upstairs . . .

"Crap."

Emma cracked her door open to find darkness waiting for her. She stepped into the hall, giving her eyes a moment to adjust. Moving slowly, her hand on the wall, she eventually found the banister. Emma paused and bit her lip as her foot lifted to the first step.

Christ, I hope this thing doesn't creak.

Her sole touched down without a sound, but she still winced during the entire climb up, expecting the cabin to betray her at every move. Near the apex, she lifted herself on her tiptoes, scanning over the top step.

Thank God. Dark. Let's hope it stays that way.

Emma went forward, unsure of where to go on a floor she'd not yet had a reason to step foot on. She peeked into a bathroom before creeping to the next door in her path. Closed, she tried the doorknob only to find it locked, but the barrier wasn't enough to stifle the reek of gun oil drifting through the cracks. It was even stronger than the smell of the workroom back home. Fine hairs rose on her arms when she remembered the huge bags her father had lugged in when they arrived.

Jesus, Dad. Did you just bring your guns or are you building your own artillery in there?

Gaze still half on the door, she moved to the last. It took her a split-second to realize it was cracked open, and she dodged away from the opening just as the first *clang!* rang out. The next came louder, the sound speeding up into a pseudo-rhythm of blows.

T-the hell?

Emma sucked in a breath and held it, sliding over just far enough to see a burst of sparks come to life in the darkness, giving her a glimpse of the back of her father's sweat-soaked shirt. The image came again, the hammer in his hand rising high over his head each time before falling to its target. She squinted, trying to angle her head for a better look, but it was impossible to see what he was striking.

The clamor finally stopped. Her father tossed the hammer aside, panting. He rose to his feet so quickly, Emma had no time to react. She stood frozen in place, while he strode out of view. Her mind screamed at her.

Move, girl! Go!

Yet she couldn't help herself. The form before her was tantalizingly familiar, even in the dark of the room. She leaned in an inch more. Her nose was almost through the crack before her eyes bulged. By then, her vision had adjusted enough to recognize a shape she helped her father install under the hood of the car only a month earlier. She backed away, her gaze still locked on what remained of the alternator sitting in the middle of the floor.

CHAPTER 10

EMMA CLOSED THE door to her room, the tiny click of the latch causing her incisors to draw fresh blood from her lip. Something between a mad giggle and a sob caught in her throat while she wiped her mouth.

He lied! He lied to me!

This time, she did laugh, soft and tittering.

And why did you think he wouldn't? That the deal was legit? He drugged *you to bring you here, for God's sake!*

Emma held her palm to her head, suddenly dizzy. Her last vain hope for her father's sanity shriveled into a little black ball. The thing throbbed inside her skull, synchronizing with the echoes of the hammer blows.

There's no way out now. There's no phone, no car. No neighbors. The best I'd be able to do is run for it.

The wind whistled past the window, dredging the overwhelming cold of her nightmares back into her bones. She clenched her teeth, trying to fight the shiver coursing through her.

Don't give up! There has to be something. Think . . .

The harder Emma tried to come up with something, the harder she struck the brick wall in her mind. She paced. *No phone, no car, no neighbors* repeated in a loop in her mind, a hopeless mantra. The words intensified to shouts, taunting her, until she ripped the book she'd been using as a calendar from the bookshelf. She tore the pages out in a frenzy, hot tears striking the paper as she crumpled them up and threw them at the wall or stomped them underfoot. Her teeth dug into her lip again, caging the scream bubbling up from her lungs.

What the fuck *am I supposed to do? Build a snowmobile from scratch? Make a goddamn smartphone out of pinecones? Or a computer out of . . .*

Emma's eyes widened.

Dad's laptop . . .

She furrowed her brow, summoning the memory of the move back into her mind. Of the bags.

Was he carrying it with all the other stuff?

The more she focused, the clearer a slim, black carrying case became in her head, camouflaged where it rested atop one of the larger bags.

Yeah . . . yeah, he was! And he wouldn't have brought it if it wouldn't work.

A creak upstairs drew Emma's attention to the ceiling. This time, there was no stopping a shudder when she overlaid the upstairs floor plan over her room.

He's in the locked room.

Fresh unease crept through her at the thought of her father meticulously checking and polishing enough guns to generate the smell she'd encountered. One by one. Piece by piece. Readying them. Despite everything that had happened, the prospect of aiming such a thing at her father still disgusted her. She'd wanted to believe her father felt the same way—that even in his twisted state, he still wished only to protect her. But now, Emma's heart clenched at just how much further he might go to do so as his degeneration continued.

An awful scene came to her of running through the knee-deep drifts outside, her panicked breaths crystallizing in front of her face until the crack of a rifle sounded like a thunderclap over the wind. Of lying in the snow, screaming, her kneecap shattered and her father standing over her to take aim at the other leg.

"Shh. I know it hurts, but this is for your own good, kiddo."

"God . . ."

Emma sat on her bed, cringing every time she heard her father move upstairs. A trace of the room's smell still lingered in her nose, tickling her nostrils. Slowly, certainty began to unfurl the knot in her gut.

I need help. He needs help. And he's not just going to let me sign on to his computer and arrange a ride out of here. Knowing him, that damn laptop probably has a password a mile long.

Hearing him clatter around up there reminded Emma of the smashed alternator upstairs. She doubted he had ever intended on such a thing at the start. Given a few more days, there was no telling what he might do next. It was far too easy to imagine him wailing away on the laptop during the next drop, their final lifeline between wilderness and society severed.

She clenched her fist, remembering the feel of the last pistol she'd fired on the range. Its weight. The recoil. A strange calm settled over her despite the impression that every bit of dust that drifted down to her was another bit of sand falling through an hourglass. The drifting motes counting down the inevitable meltdown.

I'm sorry, Daddy, but you're not giving me a choice.

"How's the bacon, honey?"

"Okay."

Emma nibbled off the corner of the strip in her hand, wishing she could cram the whole thing in her mouth. She'd never made it back to sleep, and the hunger of a missed meal had only gotten worse while she stewed. Abandoning the rest of the bacon on the plate was almost painful.

But if I let it show, this is never going to work.

Her father leaned forward, his brow furrowing.

"Did that extra sleep do you any good? You really do look a little out of it."

Emma swallowed the tiny morsel in her mouth and reached for her coffee.

"I'll be fine. You just woke me up a few times last night, that's all."

A sheepish smile crossed her father's lips that would have been charming had she not sensed the slyness in it.

"Sorry. You know I have an awful hard time stopping work on a project once I start. I'll try to keep it down for you tonight, though."

Of course. There was only one alternator for you to smash. Only so many damned guns to clean.

"Thanks."

Emma took a sip from her cup and glanced at her

father's hip when he turned to tend the next course on the stove. He'd been an advocate of concealed carry since her mother's death, and Emma couldn't remember a morning the telltale bulge hadn't been visible at his side. But now, it was absent.

I guess he's happier walking around outside with that 30.06. Thank God for small favors.

Emma examined her father while he worked over the griddle. He had a good seventy pounds on her. He was much stronger, surely, and better with a gun.

But he doesn't know what's coming.

Her thoughts turned to the locked room upstairs. While it had been dark last night, none of the other locks in the cabin were anything fancy.

I just need one minute alone up there. One damn minute. Then . . . well . . .

Emma's grip tightened around the handle of her mug, her back brushing the parka draped over her chair. Her boots and gloves waited beside the legs.

God, I hope this works.

She saw her father flip the pancakes on the griddle, raw batter sizzling. He'd made them special for her mother every Sunday.

And I really hope you don't make me do anything we'll both regret.

Emma managed to avoid wolfing down the food set before her, but just barely. She hoped the rumbling of her stomach wasn't as noticeable in her father's ears as her own while she picked at her breakfast. A tiny piece of pancake actually flew out of her mouth when she faked a coughing fit mid-chew. Her father picked the scrap up with his napkin, wincing when she went hoarse.

"Hon, you sound awful."

"Just went down the wrong w—"

Emma let the next burst of coughs drag every last ounce of crap from her lungs. She got up, letting out a halting curse on her way to the sink before hacking out a wad of phlegm. The deep breath she took afterward hurt, her chest sore from the effort. She heard her father's chair scrape against the floor.

"Em?"

Her eyes narrowed, watching him in her peripheral vision.

I always try to argue my way out of the crazy crap you want me to do, but not this time. I'll keep trying to go out there with you until you insist I stay behind.

The next breath she took came out in a gasp when her father's hand fell on her shoulder. Despite cooking only minutes earlier, his hand was so cold it almost burned. She couldn't help but pull away, rubbing at the spot like she'd just been stung. Her father looked as confused as she felt.

"I was just trying to . . . "

His hand fell back to his side, the color of the flesh perfectly normal.

How is that . . . ?

Emma shook her head, trying to dispel her father's mood and her own bewilderment.

"No, it's okay, Daddy. You just caught me by surprise, that's all." She rolled her eyes. "My own stupid coughs are making me deaf."

Clearing her throat one more time for good measure, she walked to her chair and started pulling on her boots.

Lying sucks, but I really, really hope this is working . . . for both our sakes.

Her father walked toward her, his hands up in protest despite the note of hesitation in his voice.

"Whoa. Where do you think you're going?"

Bingo.

"Well, unless you already did the whole 'securing the perimeter' thing you're so into before breakfast, I assume we're going out." She stifled another cough with her fist. "And since you insist on dragging me along, I'd rather take care of it before I drop the other lung. So, let's go already."

"I . . ."

Come on . . . the bait's right there. Take it!

Emma finished lacing up her boots and was reaching for the parka when her father lifted it off the chair.

"Never mind that. I'll take care of it. Just go back to bed and get some rest, okay? I'll bring you in some medicine before I head out."

Damn it! Why does he have to be so nice?

"I told you, I'm—"

Her father's mustache twitched in annoyance.

"Lord, you've never found an argument you didn't like! It's cold out, and you're sick. I'm your father. Now, get to *bed*."

Emma marched to her room with an exasperated sigh, muttering just loud enough to be audible. "The one freaking chance I have to get out of this place each day . . ."

Sorry, Daddy.

Pulling off the boots, she climbed into bed. Her father's footfalls reached her from the staircase, headed for the upstairs bathroom. He came back down a few minutes later with a bottle of Benadryl and a glass of water.

"Now, you stay put. I'll be back in a couple hours to check on you."

Emma gave him her best fake glare before turning away.

Yes!

"Whatever."

Emma's hand clutched the blanket a little tighter with each footstep down the hall. Her knuckles were white by the time the front door finally creaked open and slammed shut.

Hello, privacy.

Emma wanted to burst from the bed, to run up the stairs at full speed and set to work picking—or forcing—the lock waiting for her. Still, she refused to move.

This still feels too . . . easy. Either Dad feels way more comfortable than normal out here, or he's got a reason to feel confident that I can't do anything stupid while he's away.

She waited fifteen minutes before getting up, slowed by anxiety that her father was lying in wait somewhere to catch her in the act, or monitoring her on some hidden camera. Steeling herself, she pulled open her door and looked out into the hall.

Empty . . .

A quick trip back to the kitchen assured her she was alone; a trail of her father's footprints was visible in the snow outside.

And there's no way he left the keys behind.

Emma searched the drawers, hunting for anything

that might serve as a lock pick. All she came away with was a long sharpening rod. She tested its weight in her hand.

Not bad. No way it's going to open any locks, but it might be strong enough to pry the door open.

Emma headed for the stairs, feeling her heart squeezed a little more with each step up. Finally visible in the daylight, the door looked so mundane, almost inviting. She wasn't prepared for the solid *clang!* the steel made when she tried to shove the end in the doorframe.

"The hell . . . ?"

Emma rapped on the door, drawing a metallic thud from somewhere beyond the wood exterior.

Shit . . . it's just a shell!

"Damn it!"

Grabbing the steel's handle with both hands, she thrust it in the crack as if it were a crowbar, desperate for any headway. Sweat began pouring off her as she stabbed at the opening again and again, begging for even a millimeter of the point to squeeze through. A few flakes of metal drifted down to her feet.

"You bastard!"

Emma raced for the kitchen. Again rifling through the drawers, she pulled a meat tenderizer from the clutter and hurried back up the stairs. Setting the steel's tip in the aperture once more, she swung the tenderizer at the handle.

Clang!

"Open . . . "

Clang!

"The fuck . . . "

Clang!

"Up!"

Panting after a dozen more blows, she realized the steel was about halfway in. Gritting her teeth, Emma tossed the tenderizer and grabbed hold of the steel with both hands, pulling back until the tendons in her arms felt like they would snap.

Come on . . . come on . . .

The steel did its work slowly, drawing a prolonged screech from the lock before popping free. Emma spun, catching her footing right before she slammed into the wall. The front end of the steel bounced off the wood, bent into an L. Emma held the tool up, staring for a moment, before throwing it aside and pulling the door open.

Oh . . . Christ . . .

Although she'd braced herself for the sight, the amount of weaponry collected still unsettled her. AR-15s, AK-47s, shotguns, and a variety of rifles and handguns were neatly arranged on the walls as if they were mere tools on a pegboard in someone's garage. Several magazines or boxes of corresponding ammo sat under each weapon, prepped and ready to use.

No wonder Dad was huffing when he hauled all this in. Every bag he was carrying must've been ready to burst.

Emma turned, continuing to take in the sheer breadth of the armory.

And even then, some of this must've been here already.

Emma wandered to what looked like a supply cabinet. Opening it up, her gorge rose and fell at the collection of homemade pipe bombs lined up inside. Two shelves of keypads like the one on her phone were suspended over them, organized by size. Each had wires connected to a glob of putty that ran the gamut from jawbreaker to brick.

Th-that's . . . ?

A hard blink didn't erase the image before her. She swallowed and reached out with a shaking hand, barely brushing the nearest plastic explosive before she pulled back.

I really, really wish my imagination was crazy enough for me to still believe I was seeing things.

Emma slammed the door, grateful to have the explosives out of sight. She pulled a rifle—the twin to her father's 30.06—from the wall and commenced loading it. The shotguns got a baleful glance before she turned away and readied a Ruger .38 revolver instead.

At least this should only leave one hole to worry about if I really do need to use it . . .

Emma wrinkled her nose, the greasy smell of the room finally penetrating her adrenaline. She walked to the doorway and crouched, the pistol waiting in her hand.

This'll be the first place you come when you get back. To put away that rifle. And it'll probably be strapped right around your shoulder when you get up the stairs. All I have to do is wait.

Emma wet her cracking lips and readjusted her posture as the afternoon passed. Without a watch or clock nearby, she had no idea how long it had been since she took her position, but it felt like hours. Finding the door at the end of the hall as uncooperative as the one to the armory, she risked a quick jaunt downstairs to check the windows. The deep orange glow burning the horizon confirmed her suspicions.

What the hell is going on? He should've been back by now.

Emma glanced nervously back at the stairs.

What if he knows somehow? Maybe there was some hidden camera up there. Or some kind of silent alarm hooked up to a motion sensor.

Or . . . what if . . . ?

The hole in the tree line gaped in her memory.

Just . . . relax. A bobcat or coyote wouldn't go after a full-grown man, right?

Her crack about hibernation reverberated. The thought of a bear towering over her father stripped away all its humor in a hurry. Emma froze at the thought of her father lying in a drift somewhere, blood tingeing the snow collecting on his body.

"Shit!"

Emma spat the word out as if she were spewing venom before pulling her heavy clothes from the closet. Dressed, she stalked out the door, giving up the revolver for the rifle. Her father's tracks were barely visible anymore, but she knew his routine well enough to trace his steps. Huffing, she swept the perimeter at a light jog, keeping low and sticking to whatever cover she could find, still wary of an ambush if her father really had learned the truth.

Emma's legs stung with the memory of the bullets from her dream. More than once, she thought she glimpsed him through the blowing drifts, aiming at her. And then she'd picture him lying somewhere, helpless, calling for her. The disparity brought a migraine pounding behind her eyes as the images shifted and twisted into one another until neither was clear. Emma stopped at the tree line, trying to rub the pain away.

Where are you?

Looking down, she saw her father's prints were fresher, deeper. She steeled herself before tightening her grip around the trigger guard and hurrying on.

The sun continued to drop in the distance, daring her to race its descent. A cramp stabbed Emma's side with each step while she sped up, her gaze focused on the tracks until there was a glint of metal in her peripheral vision.

No!

She threw herself into the snow, fully expecting a bullet to whizz over her head. Instead, there was silence. Slowly, Emma drew her face up, lifting her rifle with it as she aimed both in the direction of the glare. In the woods. Blinking, she tried to make sense of what she was seeing.

What? I don't . . .

Shivering, Emma got to her feet, her weapon still trained on the metal flashing deep amidst the twisted trunks and branches. Her father's tracks followed before her, weaving around the thickest of the overgrowth. They ended at his rifle, the barrel snapped in half and driven a foot into frozen ground. There were no more footprints, only a tunnel of broken branches overhead that led to open sky.

CHAPTER 11

"**D**AD!"

Emma regretted calling out the moment the word left her lips. The thin trees swayed in the rising wind as if in response, the low-hanging branches whipping at her face. Through the boughs, she saw the sun was all but gone, making long shadows of the wood around her. They swam around her feet like black snakes—like the tendrils she'd seen writhing in the movie theater in her dream—waiting to ensnare and infect her. From the corner of her eye, she thought she saw one flick toward her ankle.

Emma turned and ran, breaking through the twigs and branches her father had been so careful to avoid going in. Scratched and bloodied, she fell into the snow, throwing one backward glance at the spreading darkness before dashing for the cabin.

When she reached the shelter, she slammed the door shut behind her, securing every one of the locks before retreating to the center of the room, the rifle raised in her hands. Her own breaths felt like they were strangling her before common sense intervened.

What the hell are you doing? Running from shadows? Trying to shoot *at shadows?*

Emma giggled, logic arguing with instinct and making her feel a fool. But try as she might, she couldn't relax. Every glimpse at the blackness swelling outside stirred something primal in her blood, telling her something was biding its time. Licking its chops. Swearing at the dark and herself, Emma drew the shutters.

Where did he go? Emma thought, her father's footprints padding through her head. *How did they just . . . stop?*

A gust whistled past the windows, bringing to mind the broken branches she'd seen swaying in the air.

It was like something just picked him up . . . and . . . and . . .

Emma bit her lip.

No. That's impossible. There has to be something else. Some . . .

The harder she tried to think of a reasonable explanation, the clearer the path smashed through the trees became. Either something had fallen from the sky or taken to the air, and there was nothing on the ground to account for an impact. No debris, no winged corpse, no crater.

Which means . . .

The sensation of weightlessness Emma had experienced the night before last tugged at her again as she imagined floating through the air, trying to shield her eyes while the boughs splintered in front of her until there was only freezing wind and white sky around her.

Dad . . .

Tears gathered in the corners of her eyes, fear and grief pushing them free. There had been no body, no blood, but she needed neither. Just as intuition had demanded she race the stretching shadows, it now assured her that nothing was left of her father but a memory. All 200 pounds of him. Snatched right off the ground.

Unless Dad outdid himself on the most elaborate way to screw with my head.

Emma stiffened when she remembered what remained of the alternator upstairs.

Either way, I've got no way out of here. I don't even have the keys to open half the rooms in this place. There's no computer except Dad's. No phone. No way to reach anybody.

She trembled, taking a step back as another blast of air shook the windows.

What the hell am I supposed to do?

Emma wiped her eyes, taking a deep breath before finally shouldering her rifle.

Just . . . calm down. Whatever it is, it waited for Dad to come to it. I should be safe in here. At least for now. And speaking of "safe" . . .

Emma walked to the living room, pulling up the rug hiding the safe room's trapdoor. She gave it a brief tug.

Locked and bolted. Of course. Let's see what we can do about that.

Going upstairs, Emma snatched the smallest of her father's plastic explosives from its shelf and returned to the spot above the safe room. Sweat made the plastic slick as she pressed the device against the thick door. Her index finger quivered above the crude number pad.

God, just . . . let this thing be as simple as it looks.

She gulped, steadying her right hand with her left.
One . . .
Zero . . .
ENTER!
The breath Emma had been holding came out in a gasp while she raced for cover. She hid beside the staircase, her hands clapped over her ears.
Please, don't blow up the house. Please, don't blow up the—
What sounded like a thunderclap exploded only twenty feet away, the force of the blast and its report rattling her bones. Her ears rang despite the protection of her palms, and she no sooner looked through the railing then saw the smoke billowing through the cabin.
Shit! Shit! Shit!
Remembering the fire extinguisher stored under the sink back home, she searched for its counterpart in the kitchen. A gasp of relief escaped her when she saw the red canister waiting for her.
You always did stick to your habits, Dad.
Rushing the living room, she doused the flames, sweeping the foam across the base until the fire died. Coughing on smoke, Emma went to open a window before realizing there was no way to do so.
And some of those habits really sucked.
She moved to the front door instead, her hand hesitating on the knob before finally throwing the barrier open. The wind bit her face immediately, its cold strengthened by the lack of sun. Emma squinted against it and swung the door like a fan, letting the night air howl free through the space in exchange for dispersing the smoke. She was out of breath, her arms

sore, by the time the blackness inside was finally gone. Even so, a trace of the burnt smell stuck to everything. Taking one last look at the darkness past the threshold, Emma slowly closed the door and turned the locks back into place.

She headed back to the living room, realizing she hadn't even had a chance to see if the trapdoor had been blown open or not.

It better be. I'm in no rush to try that again.

She found the door to the safe room scorched—sunken into the opening it was supposed to protect. Thick as the trapdoor was, its hinges and the material holding them hadn't been up to absorbing such a blast. Emma held her hand near the blackened metal, waiting until it cooled before shoving it down the stairs.

Descending, Emma hunted through the supplies until she found what she was looking for. Picking up the blowtorch, she tested its weight in her hands, eager to unlock whatever secrets her father kept hidden behind the last locked door—the last place she was never meant to step foot in.

Emma sniffled. Wiping her nose with her index finger, a layer of black coated the digit. Picking up the gloves and goggles, she doubted her lungs looked any better. Pausing to select a twenty-pound sledgehammer from her father's assortment of tools, she hauled her prizes up. A sigh escaped her when she looked upon the charred remains of the room her father had tried so hard to make presentable, but a certain satisfaction came with the sight, as well.

Fuck this place. It lured you here and damned you, and it's doing its level best to take me, too.

Emma had the safety gear on before she even made it up the stairs. The door to her father's room loomed at the end of the hall, waiting for her like the gateway to some lost city, begging to be breached.

I just hope you left me something useful in there. Because when I figure a way out, I'm not leaving a stick of this dump standing behind me.

CHAPTER 12

EMMA STARED THROUGH the sparks, willing the space inside the doorframe to glow a bright, molten red. Sweat slid down her forehead and past her eyes behind the goggles, blurring her progress. She didn't stop until the torch's nozzle began to sputter. Turning it off, Emma lifted the goggles and wiped away the perspiration to observe her handiwork.

Not bad, but I better make this quick. If that metal cools off, I'm screwed.

She picked up the sledgehammer resting at her feet, adjusting her stance to accommodate its weight before taking a swing at the door. The faux-wood veneer split under the blow, the metal behind it denting. Emma stumbled back, aiming her next shot. The glow inside the door was already starting to dim.

Man, I better make this count.

She huffed, reared back, and struck out with everything she had. When the hammer connected, the door flew open, crashing into the wall on the other side. Straight ahead of her, a desk rested against the far wall, her father's laptop popped open on top of it.

No way . . . no fucking way.

The sledgehammer tumbled from Emma's fingers

on her way to the desk. She tapped the ENTER key, hoping the machine would come back to life. It took her a moment to realize the device was cold, the fan off. Holding her breath, she hit the POWER button and prayed.

Just let me send one e-mail. One lousy, stupid e-mail. An instant message. A Facebook message. Anything.

Emma bit her lip while the computer went through its startup routine. The Windows logo quickly gave way to a password prompt. She hung her head. The force of gravity in the room seemed to suddenly increase, threatening to drag her to the floor.

Get over it. You knew damn well this was going to happen. Just . . . move on.

She looked over her shoulder to finally take in the rest of the space. Her father's bed lay inside one of the corners, the mattress a size too small for a man of his height and covered with the same camo blanket that rested on her own. A large bookcase lined one wall, its contents a hodgepodge of classic and paranoid— "*Survivalist*," Emma corrected herself—literature. She scanned the titles. Finding *Tom Sawyer* and *The Anarchist's Cookbook* resting beside each other conjured demented scenes of the scamp lobbing improvised explosives at Injun Joe.

Instead of making Emma laugh, the image unsettled her. It was like looking at something the two halves of her father would produce, an absurd combination blending the kind man she'd grown up with and the madman he'd become. The air blowing past the window in the room taunted her, reminding her that she'd run away instead of staying to search for him.

How the hell do you know what happened out there? Some broken branches and shadows, and you run like an idiot. Maybe he was lying somewhere unconscious a dozen feet away. Maybe something did fall and knocked him flat, and he got buried under a drift.

Emma clenched her fists, doubting herself until she remembered the broken gun.

Just . . . keep looking . . .

With nothing else to check aside from a dresser full of clothes, she returned to the desk and began searching its drawers. The first one she pulled open was filled to capacity with sheets of paper, all neatly separated by plastic dividers.

Emma took out a handful of pages and thumbed through them.

Geez, he had everything covered from DIY gardening to regional folklore. E-mails, message board posts, printouts of articles . . . there must be thousands of these in here.

Closing the drawer, she moved on to the next only to find more of the same. But when Emma opened the third, her father's face stared back at her. She picked up the driver's license. The title to the car lay under it, as did the deed to the cabin. Emma's eyes bulged at the date on the latter.

Fourteen months ago? Mom wasn't even dead yet. Did you ever even tell her about this place?

Digging deeper, she got her answer. At the very bottom of the pile, turned over, there was a photograph of her mother, her father's arm wrapped around her waist. The tip of one of Emma's fingernails tried to trace the smile on her lips. Then, she recognized the cabin standing in the background.

What the hell is going on?

Emma wracked her brain, trying to make sense of the impossible.

Mom was here. They both were. But when? When did they—

She returned the contents to the drawer and closed it by degrees, as if afraid the faintest sound would wake a ghost slumbering within.

Fourteen months . . .

She'd been fifteen then, and she'd spent part of the summer with her aunt in Massachusetts. Her parents had gone on some kind of second honeymoon. It had been a rare surprise on her father's part—as was their destination.

And Mom came back sick. She needed Dad's help just getting through the door. And even after going to the doctor she kept throwing up. Losing weight. But . . . I thought they said they went to Orlando?

The wind slammed into the window, and for just a moment, Emma thought it would blow its way in, through steel shutter and all. She swallowed, the howling outside reaching a new pitch that stuck in her head like an ice pick.

Something happened to them back then. Here. And it started this whole fucking mess. I know it.

An awful thought—a memory—settled on Emma as she thought back to her mother, recalling her final moments. She'd held her hand, trying to make sense of the silent words her lips were forming. The digits had been so stiff in her grip. Freezing.

I just figured it was shock . . .

Emma shivered, rubbing her own hand on her pants to warm it, but the recollection left the skin on her palm tingling. Frigid.

Friction didn't help alleviate the icy burn clinging to her. The sensation spread to her shoulder. Emma's teeth chattered. It was the exact same cold as her father's touch that morning.

CHAPTER 13

EMMA TOOK A seat on the floor after another few hours of scouring her father's personal effects. A mess of open books and printouts littered the floor around her. The clutter of literature and ramblings had yet to shed any additional light on the situation.

Emma's fingers dug into her stomach, the tightness in her gut making her wince.

Crap . . . I only had a couple bites to eat all day, didn't I?

She slunk back downstairs and into the kitchen. The room seemed darker than the day before, and each groan of the appliances sent her fingers fumbling for the pistol at her side. Guilt tightened around her heart like a noose when she saw the table still waiting to be set and the empty skillet sitting on the stove range.

He was here just this morning, wasn't he? Cooking for me. Trying to do something nice for me. And where the hell was I when he needed me?

Emma rubbed her head, the image of her father working the stove shifting to the one of him hammering the car's alternator into scrap. Of one where he stuck a needle in her arm. The wind renewed its assault on the windows, clawing at the shutters and sighing the frustrations of the darkness outside. She almost expected the steel to bow under the pressure.

All those crazy, awful things you did. Was any of that really you?

Emma walked to the shelves and grabbed an MRE. Tearing the pouch open, she set to work preparing something that was supposed to pass for an enchilada. Salsa roja bubbled. Remembering how badly she'd burned her mouth the first time she underestimated the power of flameless heating, she blew on her meal for several seconds before trying a bite. Her chewing slowed to a crawl once the flavor coated her taste buds. Emma glanced back at the selection on the shelves, tempted to grab something from the pressure-sealed section, but seeing her father's handwriting turned off her appetite. Still, she choked the rest of the MRE down before grabbing and uncapping a bottle of water. The container was drained in seconds.

Dumbass. If you keep letting yourself get rundown like that, you're not going to be able to think straight. And all it takes is one stupid moment . . .

To die? To get killed? Like them?

The thought of her father's body going airborne made the food roil in Emma's stomach. The memory of her mother's death mask nearly dragged the meal the rest of the way up. She kicked away the empty remains of the MRE.

But killed by what, damn it! Elves? Fairies? The ghost of fucking Bigfoot?

The empty water bottle crumpled in her hand. As the winter gusts picked up and buffeted the cabin, the two weapons she was toting felt like nothing more than popguns. She pulled her knees up to her chest, staring at the shutters.

Can whatever's out there even die?

Emma continued watching until her lids grew heavy, the rifle still around her shoulder.

Three o'clock sharp. Emma turned over, the glowing red digits burning her eyes, when the crash came from down the hall. Her parents' room.

She stumbled out of bed, her head fuzzy and still unsure of whether she was in a dream or not. Every word, every movement, felt automatic.

"Mom? Dad?"

Emma crept to her bedroom door and walked into darkness, the house silent save for the pattering of rain upon the roof. She padded down the hall until her groping hand found the doorknob. The brass and the surrounding barrier melted under her touch, pooling in the doorway. Lit by a dying lamp, the puddle bubbled at her feet until it oozed out of sight between the floorboards. Shards of glass glittered in the moonlight. Emma's gaze followed the trail of fragments to the broken window. Her mother stood before it like a statue. Clothes drenched, brown locks plastered to her shoulders, she remained motionless when a blast of air roared into the room that knocked Emma off her feet and into the wall. The cold bit through every stitch of clothing, seeping into her pores. She fell forward when it passed and struck her head on the floor. Consciousness slipping away, she lifted her face just enough to see the rain swirling around her mother in a vortex from head to toe. The nightgown didn't even flutter. Not one strand of hair moved. When the gust finally passed, the arctic air in Emma's lungs nearly choked her when she tried to speak.

"M-mom?"

Her mother tilted her head. She was still turning when everything went black. Yet Emma's other senses somehow remained awake. Remembering.

Cold washed over her like a wave of liquid nitrogen, ebbing and flowing like the tide with each creak upon the floorboards. She felt her cheek freeze to the wood beneath it. Felt the air slithering over her body with the touch of a thousand forgotten winters. The cold coated her lungs more with each breath, threatening to give the organs freezer burn by the time the footfalls finally stopped.

One of the boards groaned. A hand brushed the hair from Emma's face. From her throat. Each word escaped in a hiss, in perfect synch with the rhythm of the freezing gusts rushing into the room.

"So young. So pretty. So . . . soft."

Emma tried to move. To speak. But all she could do was listen to her mind scream.

You-you're not Mom! What are you? What the *fuck* are you?

The thing kneeling over her exhaled, the breath washing over Emma's neck.

"Shh . . ."

What lay inside the sound was absolute zero. The bottom of the ocean. The end of space. Emma heard it calling when her mother reached for her, nails tickling her jugular. The growl of a starving animal rose from the void as the jaws parted and something in her mother's face popped loose.

It didn't happen like this! It couldn't have happened like this!

Then, there came a wet sound that Emma had only heard from movie theater speakers. The growl contorted to a wheeze when the noise came again, shivering over Emma's skin before it faded out. Someone staggered. Emma thought it was her mother until her father sucked in the gasp of a drowning man. Winter went with it.

This time, Emma remembered everything when her eyes fluttered open. Her mother gazed into her face, mouth open and bloody. Remembering what had festered there, Emma didn't reach out to her. Didn't hold her.

Footfalls she had never been able to recall circled to her back. Her father's pace was steady, almost stiff. Then, there came a fleeting noise Emma had not heard before that moment but hundreds of times since: her father wiping something clean. A board just behind her creaked.

"Em . . . it's going to be okay."

"Fuck! *Fuck!*"

Emma thrashed until she scrambled to her feet. She coughed, bile burning her throat and the ceiling light searing her eyes.

All this time! All this fucking time!

Shaking, her hands wiped at her eyes then tried to massage away the pounding in her head.

You didn't want me—anyone—to know what happened to her. What you did. What she almost did.

Emma watched the light seeping through the shutters' borders.

What she must have done to you while I was out. God, no wonder you got so paranoid. If something like that could hide in Mom—in you—it could stow away in anyone.

Emma unslung the rifle from her shoulder. Walking to the window, she lifted the shutter, looking out upon the wasteland of snow and dead trees.

Maybe being so reserved held it back longer somehow. And maybe...

Emma bit her lip, remembering all the time on the shooting range, the forced reading.

Maybe . . . all that training you gave me, insisting on coming here, was only half paranoid bullshit. You wanted this thing dead, didn't you?

She narrowed her eyes at the tree line, imagining her father's broken rifle sticking out of the snow like a headstone.

And I bet you knew that meant you along with it.

CHAPTER 14

EMMA GLOWERED AT the sea of remaining paper waiting for her in the desk drawers. Sifting through the contents, she collected everything that seemed pointless and set it aside with the rest of the refuse on the floor.

Okay, fuck the DIY and paranoid stuff. Let's focus on the really *weird shit.*

Left with only her father's collection of folklore, Emma dug in. It took a conscious effort to take the material seriously, and she found her eyes rolling at more than one of the entries. Every ridiculous creature and legend she'd seen on TV seemed present and accounted for.

Thunderbirds, the Dover Demon . . . goat . . . men? With axes? Seriously?

A chuckle started up in Emma's throat and died when she thought of her father painstakingly gathering all the information before her now, trying to put a name to the thing that had festered inside his wife. Inside him.

My father, the monster killer. My father, the monster. Jesus . . .

Her mood continued to sour into disquiet the

further she went in. There were things on a few of the printouts Emma wished she hadn't seen. At one point, the eyes of a werewolf with a bodybuilder physique burned into her from an old woodcut, its jaws embedded in the midsection of a victim dangling from its hand like an hors d'oeuvre. In a black and white photo, a grim line of men in Civil War regalia posed for the camera, the winged corpse of something that resembled a dinosaur stretched out at their feet.

Emma's fingertips began sticking to the pages. She wiped a sleeve across her brow before any of the gathering sweat could slide off her face and smear the ink.

After what happened, how can I write any of this off as bullshit? How am I supposed to know a cheap legend when I've already seen evidence of something that should have been impossible?

Fresh pity welled up in her for her father, remembering the long hours he'd spent cloistered in his workroom at night.

And it wasn't just prepping food and guns. You were trying to make sense of the world, weren't you? Of what was happening to you.

Of what was done to you. To Mom.

Emma gritted her teeth, the file she was holding beginning to tear. She threw it down and started skimming through the next double-time.

Where are you, you bastard? I want your name. I want your fucking head!

The drawers emptied with increasing speed, but nothing was a match for what she'd experienced. Emma cleared 22 letters of the alphabet on the tabs before she noticed the one for "W" was nearly twice as thick as the others. Her palm struck her forehead.

Of course. Wisconsin. God, I'm an idiot.

But to her surprise, she found another name before that of the state. A subheading that covered the bulk of the files in the drawer. Emma squinted at the lettering. Her father's hand had touched the tab so many times the ink was smudged to illegibility.

Pay dirt. Finally.

She took in the name splashed in bold at the top of the first printed article, the letters tinged yellow by a highlighter for good measure. Her tongue tested the word in her mouth, letting it leave her lips in a whisper.

"Wendigo."

It felt as though the syllables had coated her face in a puff of arctic wind. She rubbed the sensation away with her palms.

Okay, found you . . . Now, what the hell are you?

Emma's earlier pace slowed to a crawl, each word branding itself into her brain in turn.

The wendigo is an evil spirit prevalent in Native American mythology. Disseminated through the belief systems of cultures populating the Great Lakes Area and Canada, the wendigo is commonly depicted either as a person who has eaten human flesh—usually as a result of starvation due to famine or an intense winter—or someone who has attracted the spirit's attention due to a kindred sense of greed. In either case, the victim becomes a receptive host for the spirit, allowing it to take possession of the body.

Emma turned the page, rubbing the phantom tickle of her mother's breath off her throat.

When fully transformed, the wendigo's host actively seeks human victims to devour, often hibernating for long periods between episodes of feeding. During this time, the creature is still fully aware of its surroundings and able to exercise a certain degree of influence over anything in its territory. This can result in anything from the blighting of crops to cursing trespassers with its own insatiable appetite. The wendigo may even guide those afflicted to commit atrocities using a measure of its own powers.

Her finger went down the page, carefully avoiding a black and white rendition of a wasted, grinning face between the blocks of text.

While versions of the creature vary, most share an affinity for cold and the ability to alter weather, immense strength, and the ability to change form. Some legends also say that the beast grows in proportion to each person consumed, resulting in a perpetually emaciated appearance, usually that of a frozen corpse. Those accused of being wendigos were typically dispatched by shattering the creature's frozen heart, followed by dismemberment and interment in sacred ground or cremation. Anything less will result in the wendigo's eventual resurrection.

The file fell to her lap.

So . . . Dad . . . Mom . . . ate someone? B-but that doesn't make any sense!

Emma's head lifted, her father's words about how he purchased the cabin echoing in her mind.

"*A hunting mishap.*"

"*Losing someone . . . like that. I can't even imagine. I really can't.*"

Emma snatched the file up, holding it as if she'd just stumbled upon the combination to a vault.

It wasn't either of you; it was him! This . . . thing . . . was already here. No one ever found a corpse. Was it . . . was it sleeping when you showed up? Was it really able to put a curse on Mom when she hadn't even done anything but show up . . . and then make it jump to another person when she died? From that far away?

Emma stared blankly at the lines of text, lost amidst accounts of cannibalism stretching from the colonial era to modern day Canada.

Christ, how strong is this thing?

Emma sighed, wishing her father was there to answer. Continuing to page through, she paused to readjust the strap around her shoulder. Her eyes widened when her hand brushed against the gunmetal, the rifle's broken twin suddenly a beacon.

Oh God . . . that's not your tombstone. You were trying to show me his.

CHAPTER 15

EMMA PERUSED THE assortment of tools lining the safe room wall with her bug-out bag in hand.

Cripes, it feels like I'm shopping in a hardware store.

Her fingers brushed the handle of an axe before drawing away and grabbing the hatchet beside it instead. She lifted the sheathed blade free of the pegboard, testing the weight with a practice swing. Satisfied, Emma pulled a roll of duct tape down and secured the handle to the side of the bag.

I just hope this'll do the job. The rifle's heavy enough on its own. The last thing I need is unnecessary weight.

Returning to the spot that had held the blowtorch, Emma propped her rifle against the wall and picked up two of the spare fuel canisters. It took a fair bit of jostling to maneuver the containers to a standing position around the bottles of water, spare magazines, and pressure-sealed meals she'd packed. Just in case. A sigh came out as she zipped the bag and hoisted it onto her shoulders.

I guess you finally rubbed off on me, Dad. I wonder if you'd be proud.

Grabbing her rifle, Emma checked the chamber and headed back upstairs to the kitchen. A quick search through the drawers produced a box of matches. She snatched it up and shoved it in her pants pocket before heading out the door.

The winter weather greeted Emma with a snarl. She gritted her teeth against the gusts and took a step outside that buried her leg up to the thigh. The wind howled, whipping snow and ice into her face until it felt like it had been shot full of Novocain. Teeth clenched hard enough to stop them from chattering, Emma kicked her leg free and pressed on toward the tree line in the distance.

Even as far gone as Dad was, he didn't deserve what you did to him, you bastard. Tears formed and froze near the corners of her eyes. *Neither did Mom.*

She tightened her grip on the gun, the outlines of the trees growing as hazy as a mirage in what were becoming whiteout conditions. There was no trace of the cabin left when she glanced over her shoulder.

I couldn't run even if I wanted to. I-I'm really going to have to do this.

Emma moved forward with new urgency, the wind stealing each crystallized breath the moment it left her lips.

It wasn't this bad until I stepped outside. It does know I'm coming.

Her teeth finally chattered in spite of aching jaw muscles. Pictures of frostbite victims flashed through her mind, the accompanying information more of her father's instructional literature. Limbs going from red, to blue, to black. Then snapping off as if they belonged to a doll rather than a human being. Emma tried flexing her fingers and toes, making sure they still had warmth and circulation enough to move.

It'll do.

Her left pinkie finger barely twitched.

I really hope it'll do.

Emma nearly crashed into the tree line before she knew she'd arrived. As hard as the snowfall had tried to drown the branches, there was no mistaking the path broken through the tight layer of overgrowth.

Almost there . . .

Emma pushed in, grateful for what little protection the trees provided from the weather. She scanned the path with each step, searching for the familiar glint of steel to guide her. Every white twig and icicle sticking out of the drifts plucked away at another nerve.

What if it's already buried? What if that thing picked it up the same way it did Dad and threw it a mile away? What then?

Her hands shivered on the rifle, fueled by more than mere cold.

Please, still be here. I'm only sixteen, and I don't want to die. I don't want all the shit that's happened over the last year to be for nothing. I don't want what happened to Mom and Dad to be for nothing.

A gust swept through the boughs and left Emma gagging on snow. Every article of clothing felt frozen to her body. Her pants actually crunched when she took her next step.

Squinting against the onslaught, her eyes widened in disbelief when she saw the ragged edge of the metal barrel sticking out of the frozen ground.

Yes! Yes! Finally!

Emma ran to the spot, ripping what was left of the

30.06 free. Shouldering her rifle, she tore the hatchet loose and started sweeping away the snow. Finding a layer of ice three feet down, she pulled off the sheath and started hacking.

Come on . . . come on . . . be here . . . you have to be here . . . !

Her arm was nearly worn out when the blade finally cracked through and split the frozen ground. A blast of cold air that shamed every gust before blew her off her feet. Emma scrambled back while freezing vapor rose in a plume. A rumble came below as the crack she'd made in the earth widened.

She pushed herself into a crouch, the hatchet raised and ready.

This is for Mom . . . Dad . . . Don't think. Don't give it time to react. Just hit the first thing you see and don't stop until it's in pieces.

The shaking stopped. From inside the hole—the grave—a wheezing sigh rose to a howl and joined the frigid breeze whipping through the trees. It was a death rattle, but there was something in the sound that made the hatchet drop an inch before Emma even realized it.

Christ . . . no . . . please . . .

Her father's eyes rose just above the edge of the hole, staring at her through points of red light no larger than a pinprick. His mouth followed, the blue lips stretched and eaten away until there was only a ragged, rictus grin. The stench of open graves wafted out on a stream of freezing air. Every bone and vein stood out through the pale, gray flesh, and as he continued to rise, Emma had to crane her head to take in all twelve feet of him, standing naked in the snow.

"D-don't move," Emma said.

She hefted the hatchet.

"I mean it!"

Pushing a massive palm into the drift beside him, the wendigo pulled a felled tree from the drift. Scraping a splinter from the bark, it began to pick its teeth. The words came out in a dead man's whisper, and even through the bitter cold that came with them, Emma could smell the rot.

"Aah, little Emmie. I thought I heard someone knocking at my parlor door. Someone . . . ripe."

Emma watched the makeshift toothpick displace something from between its incisors.

"I thought it would be more amusing if you were greeted by someone . . . familiar."

Emma watched a talon made of ice trace the lines in her father's face.

"God . . . what did you do?"

It chuckled, flicking the splinter away. Its hand moved to its stomach, a thumb stroking the deep hollow carved out below his ribs.

"Something he deserved. He should've taken your mother's place. Instead of serving me, he dared to hunt me." The thing chuckled, a nest of vipers hissing somewhere down its throat. "As if he had a chance. Or you, dear Em . . . little Emmie."

The light in the eye sockets burned a deeper shade of red.

"I had to teach your father the true order of things one mouthful at a time. Now, he understands." A black tongue wandered out of the creature's mouth like a snake, freezing to its ragged lips. The wendigo cut the end of the organ off with a flick of its claw, catching the morsel before placing it in its open maw. "And in a few moments, you will, too."

CHAPTER 16

T HE CREATURE MOVED FIRST.
Emma gawked as the fingers on the giant's hand extended. They drove toward her like the talons of some monstrous bird of prey, blotting out everything but the slices of the death head's grin between. The palm was nearly pressed against her face before she managed to react.

No!

Emma dove out of the way. She didn't see the blade connect. There was only the wet sound of skin splitting and the vibration running up her arm. Her feet kicked open air as they left the ground. A fresh blast of ice and decay gave her just enough warning to release the handle before the wendigo's teeth gnashed for her throat. The dead tree fell in the snow beside her. A slight grunt came from above while the beast wrenched the hatchet free and tossed it aside.

"That was very rude of you, Emma. You always did have lousy manners. I'll have to leave part of you in the corner for time-out."

Lying there, Emma took in the expanse of it from spider-veined legs to sunken cheeks. She felt like an ant looking up at the five-year-old about to squash it on the sidewalk.

Oh . . . fuck me . . .

The other weapons went forgotten. Emma ran and didn't look back. The thing's laughter carried to her on the wind and drilled directly in her ears.

"Go ahead, Emmie. It's not like I mind." Every word wriggled into her ear like a night crawler. "Adrenaline makes a lovely seasoning, you know. And there's nowhere worth hiding. Not here."

Emma panted, fresh panic tearing at her mind. The frigid air freezing the sweat and tears to her face.

Shit! It's right! It's absolutely right!

Emma's eyes closed, a vein in her forehead throbbing in tempo with her pulse.

So, what's it going to be, then? Hot meal, cold meal, or a bullet in the head?

Emma tried aiming her feet toward the cabin in spite of herself. The numbing cold riddling her body started to evaporate, replaced by a warm tickle that could only be the first touch of frostbite. She imagined her thumb trying to pull back the hammer on the Ruger only to snap off.

God fucking damn it!

The weather only got worse as she plowed through the drifts. Her vision was reduced to a blanket of white outside of her limbs. She finally glanced back, unable to make out any sign of the beast behind her. Any slight hope his absence caused died when an off-key humming of "Paint it Black" came to her with the next freezing blast of wind.

Still running, Emma's hand was fumbling for the 30.06 when she tripped over the front stairs to the cabin. Dragging herself up, she turned the knob and slammed the door behind her, securing every lock as fast as her dying fingers would allow. Even inside, the humming drifted through the cracks around the entryway. The gun lifted in her hands, eyes flitting to each shuttered window.

Dad underestimated this thing. None of this is going to keep it out. This place is a fucking deathtrap!

Emma looked down at the rifle's barrel in a daze, wondering what the gunmetal would taste like. She lifted the weapon, her mouth starting to open before she banged her head against the stock.

No! No, no, no! You can not *let this piece of shit get away with what it did to Mom. To Dad. People have stopped these fucking things before. You read how. You just need to find a way.*

Outside, the humming grew louder, the wind picking up strength. Several of the shutters began to creak.

Really fucking fast.

Her nostrils twitched at the smell of the gun before her nose.

The armory. The bombs!

The house started to shake by the time she reached the top of the stairs, trembling to the same rhythm digging into Emma's brain. She threw the supply cabinet open and fumbled through the assortment of explosives. Her gorge rose and fell when she spotted the largest of them pushed deep in the back, a pipe bomb wired to its side and a Post-It over the number pad. The two words on the note glared at her in thick red letters.

"LAST RESORT . . ."

Emma scooped up the bomb, still staring at the message when the roof began to groan. She looked up just as the first piece of timber snapped free and shot into the sky.

Holy hell . . .

One floor down, she heard the wooden door shatter. Metal screeched while the same wind pried the shutters loose from the wall and screamed its way in, filling the cabin. One by one, the rest of the logs composing the roof crackled and flew off, giving Emma a perfect view of the vortex swirling down to greet her.

The broken roofing twisted on the currents of the tornado. Emma sensed enough power there to lift the entire cabin off the ground, but the only winter air she felt was at her back. It blew through the door and pushed her to her hands and knees. Above, the twisting mass of snow and debris distorted to reveal the bubble around which it spun. The wendigo stood cross-armed in the eye of the storm. It leered down at her, its grin stretching the scant millimeters its ruined lips would allow. The needle teeth the smile exposed didn't belong in her father's mouth, nor did the amber saliva dribbling to its chin.

"Hide and seek was the first game he played with you, wasn't it? I thought it fitting to end on the same note."

Terrified as she was, the words brought a snarl to Emma's face.

"You fucking bastard!"

The thing wearing her father's skin wagged a finger.

"Now, now, Emmie. Language. Hmm. Yes. Your tongue does seem a fine place to start."

The wendigo's black tongue curved over its teeth, hunger the only spark in the void filling its eyes.

One wave of the creature's arm and the window around him closed. The force of the storm entered through the hole and reached for her by degrees, tugging at her.

It's just playing with me. I can't beat this thing and walk away. No matter what I do, I'm fucked.

Emma looked at the bomb in her hand.

Goddamn it all!

Setting her jaw, she pulled a match from the box in her pocket and cupped it under her hand.

You've only got one chance at this, girl. Make it count!

The flame she struck lived just long enough to light the pipe bomb's fuse.

Th-there's no going back now. God . . . help me. And please, let this work.

She crammed it into her bag seconds before the vortex carried her through the hole in the ceiling.

Mom . . . Dad . . . I'm so sorry.

The roar of the air current stole her laughter and the tears streaming down her face.

This can't be happening. I've only got seconds left. I'm going to die in seconds.

Only two thoughts gave her comfort when her father's wasted face pushed through the wall of snow, the void in its eyes gaping large enough to swallow her all on its own.

There's nothing of Dad left in that thing at all. It's so . . . hollow. So empty. Like the eye of a hurricane. All that power is revolving around nothing at all. And it's killed so many . . .

The creature grinned, the corners of its mouth quivered just below its earlobes while the second thought strengthened her.

But even though I'm about to die, too, so is he.

The creature's hand reached out and engulfed her head. The world went black, her skull trapped in ice. Then, for just a moment, everything went bright.

EPILOGUE

EMMETT KINLEY KEPT his eyes on the road.

The lush spring greenery made him want to raise the windows until the car was an airtight box. Even cloistered inside the vehicle, he fancied he caught a whiff of wet grass and lilac. His finger stabbed the button for the windows. The pressure didn't ease until the cabin appeared in the distance.

No choice but to suck it up now. I don't know why I keep comin' back here.

No sooner had the thought passed his mind than he felt like hitting himself.

Because he was your boy, damn it. And he deserves to be remembered.

Emmett punched the wheel hard enough to activate the horn.

I told him winter was gonna be bad that year. The worst in a century, I said. I told him to pack heavy to cover him and that drinkin' buddy of his when he insisted on goin'. I told him not to risk traipsin' outside when it got that damn cold. Why the hell didn't he listen?

He took a deep breath, then tried to snort out the scents he imagined he'd sucked in.

I just hope the guy who bought this place didn't forget I make these little visits every year on the day. I don't much fancy havin' my head blown off.

Lost in thought, Emmett's hand was reaching for the parking brake before he noticed the gaping hole where the front door was supposed to be. His eyebrows raised as a squirrel climbed through one of the windows and began climbing up the side of the cabin. He did a double-take at the rooms peeking at him below the charred border that should have been covered by the roof.

Oh, what the fuck?

Emmett glanced warily at the car parked beside him. Gritting his teeth, he pushed open the car door and let the fresh air enter his nose. Walking up the front steps, his fingers trembled when they wrapped around the doorframe.

"Franklin? It's Emmett. Emmett Kinley. You . . . you in there, man?"

Feet suddenly heavy, he stepped past the threshold. A opossum hissed and scampered away over a piece of steel lying crumpled on the floor. Going deeper, Emmett's mouth fell open at the sight of the scorched living room waiting just around the corner. The opossum's naked tail disappeared under what was left of the sofa.

Shit . . . I thought maybe the place got hit by lightnin', but . . . what on God's green earth? Did he try blowin' the place up or somethin'? And considerin' the guy's car is still here . . .

The last few conversations Emmett had with the man online flashed through his mind. His gorge suddenly rose.

Christ, he had a kid, didn't he?

A creak came overhead, bringing a shower of dust with it. Emmett hurried to the staircase. Remembering the animals going in and out, he stopped to scoop up a burnt table leg before he climbed the first step.

"Hey! Is there anyone up there? Do . . . do you need any help?"

There was no answer, only another squeak from the boards above. It sounded as though it had come from precisely the same spot as the last. Emmett tightened his grip on the bludgeon, splinters digging into his palm.

And if somebody's hurt, it'll take forever and a day to actually get someone all the way out here. So, it's up to me. Fan-fucking-tastic.

He placed his hand on the banister.

"I'm comin' up, okay? Just don't shoot my head off."

Emmett climbed, his legs more leaden after each step. He shivered as the hole in the roof allowed a gust to sweep down the stairs to meet him, its brisk caress defying the warm spring weather. Club held high, he took in the damage above.

The sun glared down at the remains of the second floor from a blue, cloudless sky. Emmett treaded gingerly over the warped boards under his feet, hoping the damage hadn't left them too weak to support his weight. Remembering what the interior had looked like, he couldn't help but wince at the water stains and rodent shit scattered over the place his son had loved so much.

Finding nothing but a dingy sink and shower in the first room he passed, he moved to the next.

Well, hell, you were a collector, after all.

A low whistle escaped at the collection of weapons littering the floor. Many of them were expensive, top-of-the-line models, now reduced to rust. Emmett poked his toes in, the ball of his foot eliciting a creak from the boards. Inside, something clanged against the closet lying on its side.

"Hello?"

Emmett's tongue flicked over his lips, club at the ready.

"I . . . I don't want any trouble. I just want to get a look at you. To make sure you're alright. So, if you're not a squirrel, opossum, rat, or whatever the hell else lives in here, just be cool, okay?"

Emmett went forward, his feet constantly slipping on the guns below and threatening to drop him on his ass. He was halfway across the room when the first shallow breath rasped free. The noise scraped through his ears like sandpaper, stirring the hairs on the back of his neck.

"H-hey . . . Franklin, is that you? Or . . . uh . . . his daughter? Are you Franklin's kid?"

Emmett paused at the base of the closet. He tried to sound friendly despite the tendons standing out on the arm holding the bludgeon.

"Hey, it's okay. Whatever happened, I'm gonna get you out of here."

He edged around the article's border.

"I'm gonna . . . I'm—"

He stared, lips twitching soundlessly at the face waiting for him. A red eye rolled up at him. Only hunger glimmered in the void it held. A shard of bone fell from the teeth, the skin around them shriveled past the gums. There was nothing below beyond a few cords of muscle connecting a single lung to the man's charred head. Emmett's soul withered as he watched the organ pump without blood. Without a heart.

"No . . . It can't . . . It looks . . . it looks just like . . .

A wheeze hissed out between the dead man's jaws. As they parted, an unnaturally long, black tongue slipped out and scraped the floor, dragging the head toward Emmett like a snail lugging its shell. The foul stench of corpses rose from its grinning mouth, a fresh gust rising to Emmett's nose each time the tongue slapped the boards.

He took a step back, his left hand clenching the table leg just below the right. Lifting the club with a scream, Emmett swung the weapon with enough force that the burnt skull shattered on the first blow.

Emmett stood there, panting, weeping. He was still trying to catch his breath when the next gasp took him by surprise. Freezing air pushed its way into his mouth even as he tried to cough it out, filling him until he was sure he was going to pop. A winter storm whispered to him from the inside and coated his every bone with ice.

"Such a large family you have. And so very, very sweet . . . "

The cold wind that blew through Emmett's bones told him spring was over. And for him, it would never come again.

THE FEAR MERCHANT

THE JACK-O'-LANTERN ON Roy Wallace's porch was in desperate need of a Botox treatment. A mere week after Halloween, rot was already hard at work on the toothy grin. The corners of its mouth had drooped into a grimace, and the gourd reeked of sweet decay and old smoke. His face twisting into the same mask of displeasure, Roy didn't know what to blame: the odor or the house across the street.

DiStefano . . . how am I supposed to compete with that prick?

He considered ending his creation's torment with a boot through the face as he looked upon the parade of children passing through his neighbor's door.

Damn, they're still going over there? The line looks even longer than it did an hour ago.

Roy hissed out a sigh to match the one blowing through the dead leaves on his doorstep.

I haven't seen those piled up in twenty years.

He could almost feel DiStefano rubbing his nose in them.

Fucker got his first visual effects Oscar the same year I washed out of FX school. Always on top while I've been at the bottom.

His teeth gritted while he watched the kids walk slack-jawed past the animatronic werewolf peering down from the roof. One of them shrieked as the jaws snapped shut overhead before opening again to howl. The cry wasn't loud enough to distract Roy from the pad of sneakers on his lawn. The sound got a half-smile out of him.

"Hi, Richie! You come back for another visit?"

Richie, awkward at twelve, kept his sights on his feet and still managed to trip over them. He barely caught the railing.

Is it really getting that hard to look me in the eye?

"I just came to return the candy tray for Mom on my way to . . . "

The boy's gaze flitted across the street. If Roy's teeth were clenched before, they were now just shy of cracking. He took a breath to calm himself.

"Mr. DiStefano's? You've already been over three times since Halloween. Haven't you seen everything already?"

The boy's face reddened as he extended the tray to Roy, but he was racing back across the lawn the moment he completed his duty. A few shouts over his shoulder proved all the attention Richie had left to pay his old hero.

"Sorry, Mr. Wallace, but there's no knowing how long he'll keep everything up! You really should come over at least once! You wouldn't believe some of the stuff he's got in there!"

The words echoed in Roy's ears while he watched Richie disappear laughing beneath the lycanthrope. He brushed a thumb over his stubble.

The kid's got a point. Why not check out the

competition while I still have the chance? It'll be like research for next year. No, recon.

Slowly, stiff-backed, he made his way across the street.

The natural bubble that divided adults from children allowed Roy access to the door ahead of his place in line. The few kicks and curses aimed his way went ignored as he walked beneath the werewolf's jaws.

Although he'd seen dozens of children enter the doorway, he was totally unaware that a sort of tunnel stretched beyond the opening. He could not see the end when he ventured forward amidst the crowd.

Body heat and preteen B.O. stifled him while he struggled to find his way. Perhaps warped by the temperature, the rubber composing the floor of the tunnel became almost mushy underfoot.

The smell grew worse.

None of the children seemed to notice as they shouldered their way ahead. Instead, they squealed with delight while they pointed to shapes in the darkness Roy could not make out. He squinted into the murk.

I can't see a damned thing. What's everybody getting so worked up for?

He rubbed his eyes, trying to get used to the gloom. When the shadows finally lifted, the cobwebs littering the hallways became no more fearsome than strands of tinsel.

Jesus . . .

Ice raked his innards as the bulbous form on the ceiling leered at him and cocked its eyeless head. Human teeth chattered behind a set of mandibles longer than his arm. Each snap of the jaws punctuated the wave of screams passing through the crowd. Roy's lungs seemed to shrivel each time the cries reached a higher pitch. The world went fuzzy while the tangle of human limbs protruded from the bloated brown body and gripped the walls. He could feel the children pressed against him trembling.

Roy's nose tingled with a mélange of latex and machine oil the same moment the first nervous chuckles erupted around him. The children applauded when the appendages anchoring the creature to the roof of the tunnel finally carried it out of sight. It was only when the machine turned and allowed Roy a clearer look at its face through strands of dangling black hair that he remembered and let his breath escape.

That . . . that was the monster from Curse of the Spider People. *The one the lead turned into at the end. And—I remember now—that furball outside was from* Crescent Moon.

Heat warmed Roy's face when he realized he hadn't seen anything new since stepping foot in the house. The same smell that had wafted from the first animatronic perfumed the space, speaking of fresh grease on old, steel limbs. He shook his head, getting more pissed by the second.

This isn't a haunted house; it's a goddamned shrine to his own career! He'll probably keep it open all year-round. Stroking that big Hollywood ego.

"Prick. Goddamned *prick!*" Roy whispered in a sputter when he again coaxed his feet to move. Any fear still lingering inside him quickly gave way to rage. He identified each of his rival's creations as they came into view, punctuating each name with his spit.

"Terrok—*The Demon's* Tomb! Jerrod Leech—*Beneath the* Floorboards!"

Every step confirmed his suspicions. Nothing was new. It was all recycled, all professional, and all of it horrendously expensive.

I can't compete with . . . with this! Not now, not ever.

The names came faster as beads of light started to spin within the tunnel, their illumination masking the robotic motions of DiStefano's party favors. Only the occasional screech of rusting gears betrayed the illusion. Roy barely kept his balance while the children yelled to each other and doubled their pace in anticipation of seeing more.

Perhaps it was from being crammed between so many bodies, but the tunnel seemed to shrink. Yet the props somehow kept up with the onlookers despite the lack of space. A new one popped up with every couple of steps.

Enough of this . . . I'm done.

Johnny Walker called for him from the liquor cabinet back home. The lights were becoming a blur, blazing brighter with each movement. The smells of perspiration and rubber tickled his gag reflex through his nostrils.

Roy thought to turn, but knew it was impossible before he even started. The mob of children was already squeezing him. There wasn't much more than an inch between the bodies behind him. He gritted his teeth and used his size to press forward instead.

Come on, come on! Let's speed this thing up!

A cruel jolt of satisfaction came when the toes of a sneaker flattened underfoot.

Little traitor. Serves you right.

Bitter and dejected as he was, the anger died when he realized the squeak of pain that followed belonged to Richie. He suddenly felt far uglier than any of DiStefano's props.

"S-sorry," he said, placing his hand on the boy's shoulder. "It's kind of hard to keep track of your feet in here, y'know?"

Instead of the mutter of acknowledgment he was expecting, Roy heard only something like a hiss aimed in his direction. The boy's flesh vanished from beneath his hand as though he were a ghost. Roy looked over the sea of heads, but Richie was nowhere to be seen.

Shit, what the hell was that *about?*

The noise stayed with him when the mob finally turned a corner in the tunnel. The new corridor was narrow and slick underfoot, and worse yet, the sound seemed to echo under the clamor of the children.

I . . . I must've missed an animatronic somewhere, that's all.

Roy's eyes searched for a source, but DiStefano seemed out of tricks. The passage was now only wide enough to accommodate a single-file line, and the ceiling was mere inches from his head. Even the children were silent. Light burned ahead.

The exit. Oh, thank God.

Roy wondered just how large DiStefano's house actually was. It felt as though he'd walked miles, his sense of time warped.

Roy walked through the outline of light, expecting a breezeway or perhaps a white porch, and instead found the one thing he was sure DiStefano couldn't throw at him—something entirely new.

Ahead of all of them stood Clark DiStefano himself, his messy hair and black moustache the same as in every horror magazine feature. There was no mad rush to greet him as each child walked forward and clasped his hand. Indeed, their body language betrayed more exhaustion than excitement. When they passed their host, some of them actually staggered en route to the peculiar round door that was the true exit of the place.

Roy had plenty of things to say to the man, but they all fell from his tongue when he noticed the first child fall in a stupor at DiStefano's feet.

That's Jess Harper! Did she faint? Does she need an ambulance?

Roy tried to pass the girl in front of him only to bang his shoulder. The whiteness of the room gave it an illusion of size, but it was every bit as narrow as the passageway preceding it. Desperate, he tried to pull the child ahead of him out of the way.

Roy cried out when the little girl's nails raked the back of his hand. He nearly struck her out of instinct, but his palm froze the moment she turned around.

Her eyes were as white as the room.

It's just the lighting. It has *to be the lighting . . .*

Roy stumbled back. The same horrid screeching of gears assaulted his ears. He was trying to claw the sound out when two tiny hands pushed him back into place. They were far stronger than they should've been. Worse than the ones that had bruised him up during his one and only mosh pit. One more shove and he was back in line.

The little girl covered the gap between her and the next child in a sort of sleepy jog, her head dipping as if she were about to fall asleep. DiStefano chuckled when she tottered over the instant she touched his hand.

Roy paused too long, and this time, he was thrown rather than shoved. His chin cracked against the floor while he lay face-to-face with the girl. Her eyes were still open—still white—but he couldn't tell if she was breathing. It took him a moment to notice the handkerchief wiping the blood from his face.

DiStefano smiled beneath his moustache as he used his free hand to dust Roy off.

"Did you like it?"

Roy struggled to stand and fell back to his knees.

"You . . . what are you—?"

"Doing to them? To you?" DiStefano asked with a cock of his head. "Just a little tradeoff." He leaned closer to Roy's face. "You see, I'm retired, but I can't give up the rush. The *fear*."

DiStefano folded the handkerchief up and returned it to his shirt pocket. "Do you know what it's like to feed off the fear you sow for years just to have your services no longer en vogue? All that CG crap nowadays? Pheh! There's not a bit of fear in it! And do you know why?"

DiStefano's breath whistled in Roy's ear. It burned inside his head like liquid nitrogen.

"It's because no *hands* have ever touched it." DiStefano flexed his fingers as if there were a puppet dangling below. "It's all computer programs. They've lost the soul a craftsman puts into his work. And vice-versa, I've lost the thrill it brings me when it scares the hell out of someone.

"They," he said, motioning to the girl, "will come back time and time again without remembering this part of the experience. They're children. They live moment to moment. You, however, are a *concern.*"

Roy gasped as DiStefano took his hand. The effects master's lips didn't move, but his voice snickered in Roy's brain.

And—I hate to tell you—an amateur, at best.

The white room faded with the echo. Alone, Roy found himself back in the tunnel through which he first entered the house.

What . . . ? How . . . ?

Regaining his balance, he moved drunkenly beneath the spinning lights. As Roy tried to shield his eyes, he saw DiStefano's monsters had returned, as well.

This time, their fluid movements were no trick of lighting. They slithered and clawed their way from the walls and ceiling that once sealed them, their teeth and pincers trained upon the spy revealed in their midst.

Roy whimpered as each set of jaws released the same horrid, hissing sound before clamping on his flesh. The noise was far worse than anything DiStefano's puppets had produced—more primal than a Foley artist's wet dream. It mingled with the crunching of bones and the sloshing of innards.

It reminded him of pumpkins.

BANG!

RICHARD SWAYED IN time with the piano music seeping up to him through the roof. The vibrations tickled his feet through the soles of handmade Italian shoes, as did the conversations of the diners still inside the restaurant—and their heartbeats. Elongated ears trembled at the sound of the door opening below. He grumbled in tune with his stomach at the sight of the couple walking out arm in arm.

Wonderful. Another pair of bloody lovebirds.

Richard pulled a silver pocket watch from its place in his vest.

There are only four people left inside and dinner service ends in fifteen minutes. His stomach growled even louder than before. *If I have to skip another meal, so help me . . .*

Five minutes passed before fresh footfalls sounded below—the remaining patrons all leaving the same table. He waited while they exited to the sidewalk and said their goodbyes. Two cars roared to life and buzzed down the street. Aching from the cacophony, Richard's ears still picked up the click of high heels on cement. He smiled, the stinger under his tongue twitching.

Finally.

He waited until the woman was nearly across the street before peering over the ledge. She was young, perhaps mid-twenties, her dark hair worn up fashionably to show off the platinum and emerald necklace draped around her throat. The gem's color matched her dress. Drawn by the thrum of the pulse under the stone, Richard leapt weightless—soundless—to the roof of the building she'd just passed.

The music of the woman's body came to him clearer while he shadowed her from above, interrupted only by the inane ring tone of her cell phone.

Healthy. A pleasant blood type. And a glass or two of Malbec to add a bouquet to the whole repast. Lovely.

The street sounds quieted with his approach. Thick shadows already stretched along the woman's path condensed into a murk behind her, hiding Richard's descent to street level. The scarce light still around her shrunk until he was nearly on top of her. Richard took a moment to savor the confusion on the woman's face when she looked up from her phone, his hand already reaching for her through the darkness.

I'm sorry, my dear. It's nothing personal. Just consider this a stroke of ill luck.

Nearly brushing her skin, Richard recoiled when a force rocked the woman off her feet. She lay at his feet, a dribble of blood running from her scalp to the bridge of her nose. Richard stiffened, a familiar snuffling just audible deeper in the murk. He whipped in its direction just in time to see a hairy arm poking through the shadows—*his* shadows—jagged talons stretching toward his prey.

Richard latched onto the woman's ankle before the claws could touch her, leaving them to rake the concrete. He hissed his rage into the murk.

"Troy! I know that's you in there, you miserable scavenger. Show yourself!"

A coarse chuckle followed his rival through the gloom. Broad-shouldered and sporting a slight beer gut under a flannel shirt, Troy smirked, the edges of fangs resting over his lips.

"So what, you English turd? You wanna finally do something about it? Huh? You up to it?"

"Always." Richard released his prize and stood to face his opponent with his pale chin in the air. Troy dropped to all fours, the growl of a feral dog rumbling deep in his throat. Richard slid into position to sidestep and parry the lunge he knew was coming. Both waited, bodies tensed, until an approaching siren killed the mood.

"Gawddammit all!" Troy snatched the woman's wrist, dragging her until Richard made a diving leap for her ankle. They stood there, deadlocked, while the siren drew closer. "Let go, you fucking ass pain!"

Richard's claws drew blood from the woman's leg. The warmth kissing his fingers only tightened his grip. "Never."

Troy licked his chops, gaze flitting toward the dull red and blue lights growing brighter in the distance. "Well, I'm not letting go, either, so what the hell do we do now?"

A glint below drew Richard's attention to a shape gleaming in the woman's purse. A tight smile cut his lips. "We settle this as we should've months ago. Tonight."

Richard crossed his legs under the card table in Troy's garage. The last traces of the sirens they'd evaded died beyond the back alleys—overtaken by the termites foraging in the innards of the moldering bungalow. Bound and gagged, the woman wriggled in rhythm with the insects, as if all had the same inkling of what was to unfold.

And so it begins . . .

Richard's finger stroked the .44 caliber round before sliding it into one of the six vacant holes in the Colt Anaconda. He matched glares with Troy while the same finger spun the cylinder, allowing it to turn for a full second before shoving it back into the gun. Taking a deep breath, Richard lifted the barrel and placed the muzzle against the side of his head. His thumb cocked the hammer. A tremor in his index finger helped him pull the trigger.

Click.

A growl of disappointment came through the slight gap between Troy's front teeth. He pushed several locks of greasy black hair away from his eyes as the revolver was placed on the table and spun around before being pushed his way. "Lucky bastard."

"We'll see."

As Troy picked up the weapon, a flicker of disgust came into his expression while he examined the pink grip. His pupils, slits, widened to orbs when the woman bound and propped against the wall tried to speak through the gag in her mouth. He lifted the gun's barrel between his thumb and forefinger as if he were embarrassed to even be seen with the thing.

"Pink? Really, lady? You do know this is for killing, right?"

Richard sighed although he agreed with the sentiment; his opinion of the revolver was about the only thing he could recall ever agreeing with Troy about. "Please, get on with it."

The pupils slimmed to their original shape when Troy returned his gaze to Richard. Flipping the weapon end over end in the air, Troy caught the Colt, put the muzzle against his head, and pulled the trigger.

Click.

Troy chuckled, the laughter pulling his thick lips just far enough back to expose the extra row of teeth hidden beneath the one in front. His clawed hand shoved the gun across the table hard enough to strike Richard's abdomen. "Your turn."

Richard grimaced as he picked up the revolver, the long, well-manicured talons on his own fingertips a far cry from the chipped cuticle tapping on the other end of the table. Yet again, he wondered if the woman they were fighting over was even worth it. She'd seemed so appealing in the darkness when he'd stalked her, but under the light of the bulb in Troy's garage, she looked almost too scrawny to be worth the trouble.

Watching Troy blow a hole in his own head on the other hand . . .

"Come on!" Troy said, his voice becoming even more guttural as it failed to filter his excitement. "Do it!"

The grin had stayed plastered on Troy's face, and it spread farther when Richard returned the muzzle to his temple.

Click.

"Hard luck," Richard said. Not so much as a quick smile passed over his lips. The grinding of the gunmetal against the wood hurt his ears, but he kept his poker face intact. Troy was far easier to read, his smirk gone the moment the weapon failed. Richard was tempted to warn his opponent to restrain himself when Troy snatched the weapon up. The inner workings of the Colt groaned under the pressure of his rival's grip.

"You've always been a tight-assed wad," Troy said. "From the first day you showed up in that thousand-dollar suit with your stupid accent, staking out all the high-class meat in town. Well, you're going *down!*" A growl started in his throat, rising to a roar as he shoved the Colt's muzzle into his mouth.

Click.

Troy pulled the barrel from his mouth, panting. The smirk had returned. "Fifty-fifty odds. Good luck with that." Clearly knowing how much the friction between the weapon and the table bothered his opponent's sensitive hearing, he prolonged the contact before sliding the weapon back to Richard.

Richard didn't bother remarking on the tactic, although his ears had all but screamed. He gave Troy one long and calculated stare, from tattered flannel shirt to the dandruff on his scalp before allowing his eyes to settle again on the cat-like slits.

Thank the Darkness I had better breeding. I'd sooner eat my own tongue than look at that wretched, inbred face another night. Perhaps I'll take a trip home after this is all over to cleanse all this hick culture from my palate.

He lifted his head and placed the Colt's muzzle under his chin.

Click.

The splintered edges of Troy's fingernails bit into the surface of the table when the revolver slid back to him and brushed his knuckles. His voice was thick with hatred while he hefted the weapon, baring both sets of teeth.

"Prick!"

Richard watched his opponent glance back to the woman, silently damning her for the humiliation she'd indirectly caused him. The woman's brown eyes grew massive beneath her plucked eyebrows as Troy placed the Colt's muzzle against his head. A ghost of the smirk returned when his thumb pulled back the hammer.

"I hope you choke on the bitch."

Bang!

Richard watched Troy's head jerk, the power of the magnum round blowing out the back of his opponent's skull. There was no mistaking the sound coming through the woman's gag as anything else but a scream while blood and brains splattered across the floor behind the chair. Smoke rose from the Colt's barrel and both ends of the wound as Troy's head lolled back between his shoulders.

How did I know you'd leave a mess?

Richard left the table and walked to his opponent's side, waiting. Minutes passed. Slowly, Troy lifted his chin. Blood dribbled from his eyes. Pushing himself up, more splashed across the table as he spoke. Every syllable sounded pained.

"Fine! Take it! Take her! I don't need this place! Everyone knows they're fatter down south, anyway!"

Richard sighed and admired the sheen of his claws. "You *would* equate weight with quality." He walked to the woman squirming on the ground and slung her across his shoulder. "You have twenty-four hours to leave town. Should you linger longer than that . . ."

"Yeah, yeah, I know." Troy turned his head to allow him to better rub his wound. Richard could see tissue growing inside the cavity. The following layers of bone, flesh, and hair would take days to fully return.

As Richard began to walk out, he heard Troy call after him, the effort making his opponent's already guttural voice a gargle.

"Maybe you're right! Quality over quantity, eh?" A coughing fit erupted behind Richard when he grabbed the handle of the garage door. By the time the door was lifted enough to provide an exit, the sound was close to laughter.

"Screw the south!" Troy croaked. "I think I'll try some English food instead."

Richard's poker face finally broke, his upper lip trembling at the thought of Troy invading his motherland. Breeding. He let the garage door drop behind him and carried his victim into the shadows. As the woman kicked uselessly against his undead flesh, Richard felt a knot tightening in his guts.

Walking into the darkness, Richard paused. He flexed his jaw, the stinger slack under his tongue.

Blast it all!

He hefted the woman to the ground, slashing through the woman's bonds with one deft motion of his hand before grasping her face. Shadows squirmed behind her eyes, eating her memory of his features. Richard pulled the gag from her mouth.

"Be on your way, miss. And don't you dare scream."

She stared his way, blinking rapidly to clear the haze he knew hovered over her eyes. Grumbling, he set her back on the direction she'd originally been going. Something between a sob and a hiccup escaped her lips.

"Th-thank you. But why are you . . . ? I thought you were going to . . . I mean . . . "

"Eat you?" Richard sighed, patting her shoulder before giving it a push. "Well, even monsters can lose their appetites, my dear. And right now, all this one wants is a drink."

LITTLE RED VEST

KATHY SULLIVAN GROANED in tune with her car's engine.

Come on. Oh, come onnnn . . .

Her hands tightened around the wheel while she pushed the Lexus to the nearest space on the side of the road. The vehicle barely squeezed in before sputtering its death rattle. Karen's head banged against the wheel.

A year and a half since my last vacation and the car dies on day one. Of course. Why not?

She got out and slammed the door behind her. The ivory paint reminded her of the dealer's bleached teeth.

Like brand-new, ma'am. Full package. Very reliable. She banged a fist on the roof. *Asshole!*

Kathy fished for the cell phone in her purse, praying AAA had someone close by.

Just stay calm. You can get a cab to get you to the hotel. Big as this city is, there's got to be a mechanic around who can get that piece of junk running again by the time this little trip is over.

Realizing she would need to give the person who answered her call a location, she looked around, but nothing rang a bell. Kathy choked out a few notes of bitter laughter.

I guess that's what I get for swearing loud enough to drown out the GPS.

She repositioned the sunglasses on her nose, the August sun forcing her to squint behind the lenses as she looked for a street sign. Kathy retreated into the shade offered by the buildings. She could just make out a sliver of green a few dozen yards down the street. With a disgusted sigh, she dropped the phone back into her purse and braved the summer heat.

Faded signs and graffiti accompanied her on her walk. The architecture was old, crumbling, and she felt a pang of sadness that so little care was paid to something that should have been charming. There didn't even seem to be a theater or nightclub around to offer any entertainment, only bars, and stores missing too many letters to give any idea as to the wares obscured behind the grimy windows.

Crap . . . I've never been in the area by the hotel, either. Those reviews and photos on the website better be the real thing or I'm making two calls to the Better Business Bureau when I get back.

Kathy picked up her pace and her feet, as if fearing she might somehow fall into one of the cracks in the sidewalk. It was far too easy to imagine her younger face looking back at her from the windows. She bit her lip.

You are not *Mom and Dad. You don't work two jobs for peanuts. You don't have overdue rent payments. And you're not going to have a heart attack and die nose deep in a pile of someone else's laundry. You busted your ass and made something of yourself. This is someone else's hole. You. Got. Out.*

A clean swath on the glass reflected the same bags that lived under her mother's eyes. She looked away to find locals pushing creaking doors open to crowd her on the sidewalk. Kathy sucked her teeth when the nearest handle grazed her elbow.

Ugh, and I thought the buildings around here were a mess.

After a decade of living well, the ripped jeans and dirty work boots worn by the residents brought more bad memories of her old neighborhood bubbling to mind. Pretty even pushing thirty-two, her clothes new and in style, Kathy knew she stood out like a movie star in a whore house. She squirmed, trying to will the hem of her skirt down farther when she caught a few appraising looks from the men walking by. Some of the women glanced over their shoulders. They were still close enough for her to hear the snorts of derision aimed her way.

Kathy's hand was in her purse up to the wrist by the time she made it to the sign. The sensation of the Taser's plastic handle in her palm soothed her fears.

All you have to do is get the street name and get back to the car. Then, you can seal yourself in, lock the doors, and try to forget where you are until the truck shows up. She looked up. *Just past the corner of 23rd and Beaumont. Beautiful.*

Kathy had already turned, her heels clicking on the cement, when her ears began to ring. The hand unattached to the Taser rose to her head and tried to rub the sound away. As it faded, music took its place.

What . . . is that? Some kind of show?

Kathy couldn't place the notes. The piece was instrumental, its style something that might have originated in a dance hall near the turn of the twentieth century. Short bursts of fuzz occasionally interrupted the lively tempo, indicating a scratched record or defective disc at work. Yet, the melody that reached her didn't sound as though it were coming out of any kind of modern speaker. The music was richer somehow. Warmer.

I can't believe it, but that . . . actually sounds amazing. Way too good for this place. Maybe I could take a little peek and see what kind of instrument it is. At least that way I'd get something worthwhile out of this mess . . .

Her teeth worried her lower lip before she decided to turn. When she did, she found all those who had passed her walking in the direction of the sound. Her fingers stayed around her weapon as she followed.

Just stay cool. Nobody wants to screw with you. They obviously want to take in the same performance you do.

Kathy saw a few heads bob near the front of the line. The music tickled her ears like a lover's lips. Every whisper coaxed her farther on.

The closer she got to the crowd forming in front of her, the more her confusion grew. She had sensed the weight of aches and bitterness weighing the inhabitants down before. Now, they were cheerful, laughing amongst themselves. Some of them were even humming along with the tune. A final moment of indecision came as Kathy followed them to the mouth of a back alley. She hung back while the people in front of her squeezed into the opening. The scents of sweat and cheap perfume lingered behind them even when she found room to slip inside.

This part of the walk was mercifully short. No more than ten seconds passed before the sun's heat was drawing fresh perspiration from her forehead. The music was very loud now, almost deafening. Short as she was, she had to circle around most of the crowd and thread her way into the front row to get a good look at its source.

The mob had led her to a vacant lot. Grass and weeds poked through the cracks in a layer of asphalt that must have been laid nearly a century ago. The foundation of a building sat cradled at its core like a rotten heart. Only the first floor remained standing, hollow, amidst the scattered debris of the higher levels. In its shadow, an organ grinder madly spun the crank of his machine.

The fellow was clad in black pants a size too small and a white shirt with its sleeves rolled up to the elbows. A muzzle of short gray hairs peppered his round face. Already rocking in sync with the tune, the grinder began to dance.

The crowd clapped along to the rhythm.

The fellow came closer, his body managing a mad jig badly at odds with the beat of the music he played. Kathy backed away when she saw the exhaustion on the man's face. Sweat was pouring down his scalp and over his eyes, probably all but blinding him as he continued his performance. Looking around, Kathy saw some members of his audience begin to mimic his movements, dancing close enough to drop a coin into the little container fixed to the top of the organ. The grinder danced more wildly with each donation. His extra effort brought Kathy's attention to the soles threatening to tear loose from his shoes.

The crowd began to chant. "More!" they shouted. "More! More!"

What do they want? Blood?

But to Kathy's surprise, the man didn't increase the speed of his feet any further; he stopped—all but the hand making the music. Reaching the other over his shoulder, he carried something forward.

Kathy thought it was a monkey at first. One of those cute, white-faced Capuchins one might see hanging off a street performer in an old movie. The little red vest it wore was a dead match. However, as the creature crawled down the grinder's hand and onto the organ, she saw it had no tail. There was no fur. Only pale, hairless flesh.

W-what . . . is . . .

Kathy's hand squeezed the Taser until the casing threatened to crack when the organ grinder's pet reared up on its hind feet. As it looked at her, an idiot grin greeted her stare. The little beast's massive square teeth formed a yellow, half-moon smile nestled between jug ears. The thing began to dance.

Kathy could not look away while it cavorted and flipped, bare feet slapping on the chipped surface of the organ as it continued the show. All the while, the grinder turned the crank with a speed that should've made his wrist cramp, increasing the tempo to a level that transformed the piece he played from spirited oddity to freak show symphony. Then, everything began to change.

A thin mist rose from within the ruins behind the organ grinder, stretching skyward as it spread. The scent of fresh concrete blew to Kathy's nose on a breeze. Shimmering like a mirage, the building that had gone to ruin loomed over the neighborhood once again.

Kathy rubbed her eyes.

That's impossible! All of it! I'm seeing things. Got to be.

But the building was still there when she looked again, even more details coming into focus while the grinder played on. Sun glinted off long, shattered windows, and a pigeon fluttered down to rest on one of the outcroppings. Even the cracks in the pavement around the building seemed to be healing, drawing tight as if they'd been sutured shut by the fog.

More people came forward, allowing the creature to pull coins and bills from their hands. Some even laughed when the thing leapt to their shoulders or danced on their heads before jumping back to its master. Meanwhile, the crowd pressed closer, carrying Kathy with them. She flinched when the creature landed on the purse of the woman next to her. While it climbed up the strap, the grin found Kathy again, as did its eyes. The pupils held black slits in twin pools of piss, but they widened to circles when she finally found the voice to scream.

"Don't look at me!"

The music stopped, the phantom building fading to a wisp with the last echoes of the notes. Slowly, as if waking from a trance, the onlookers turned their eyes upon her. The smiles and laughter melted from their lips, replaced by a cold hatred that made Kathy pull the Taser free. She said nothing as she backed into the alley. Neither did the spectators. They only watched.

Stop . . . stop looking. Just leave me alone.

The darkness around her provided no comfort. The

sweat escaping Kathy's pores dotted her skin like chips of frost, and a chill worked through her as a summer breeze blew into the alley.

Kathy tried to remember if there was any obstacle she might trip over. She was far enough away from the audience to risk a look behind her, but the figures frozen at the end of the passage transfixed her sight. The onlookers were bathed in shadow despite the sunlight she knew was scalding them. Ebony statues, they did not move when the organ grinder returned to his performance.

The notes came without warning. A few slow turns of the crank were enough to paralyze her. Each beat brought a vibration trembling through Kathy's brain. Something sticky trickled from her ears as the sensation worked its way down along her spinal column, seeping into her nerves. Her body trembled, refusing her command to run.

God . . . what's happening . . . to me?

Kathy could only watch while the organ grinder's pet hopped from man to man, stopping to grin at her from atop the shoulder of the spectator closest to the alley before leaping to the ground. The creature approached her on all fours, its course bringing its side scraping against the brick wall beside it. The little beast placed a hand against the border in mid-stride, each extremity following until it walked along the masonry.

The creature stopped about a foot in front of her. She was unable to move when it jumped for her head. The thing's strange eyes and half-moon smile formed a new and even more hideous visage as it looked into her face upside-down. Slowly walking down her arm, it stopped to inspect the Taser still clutched in her fingers.

Get off me . . . Get the fuck off me!

Kathy's whole body felt like it was stuck somewhere between being devoid of circulation and the prongs of a tuning fork. All her efforts barely earned a twitch. Still, she focused her will on her index finger as the abomination resting on her arm leaned in close enough to sniff the electrodes.

Her vision swam when an arc of blue light flashed at the end of the Taser. She convulsed as the creature shrieked, its nails digging into her wrist hard enough to draw blood while the current coursed through its body. Kathy fell forward, the beast releasing a final anguished squeak before her weight crushed it under her chest.

Kathy lay gasping, twitching, as the spectators entered the alley. Someone grabbed her roughly by the back of the neck, lifting her high enough to extract the bleeding mass underneath her before dropping her back to the ground. No one else disturbed her while the marching feet passed around her and left their echoes trembling in her bones.

From where she lay, she could see the organ grinder standing where she'd left him. He was too far to make out the expression he wore when his hand abandoned the crank. Kathy didn't have the strength to make it to her knees when the grinder stepped into the alley and crouched beside her head.

Again he began to play, the rhythm pumping directly into her ear canal. The sound entered her mind and spun the contents like a whirlpool. Calm, cold, she began to lose herself in the tide. As the world disappeared, the last thing Kathy saw was the organ grinder's hand laying a little red vest beneath her nose. Her nostrils tingled, picking up traces of the same detergent her mother used to reek of through the blood and animal musk. A gruff voice echoed with the music in her head.

"Break time's over. Now, go and scrub that clean."

SHADOWPLAY

CALEB HUNTER RESTED his elbows on his desk. The small white carton of pork lo mein that rested between them had been empty for almost fifteen minutes. As usual, the remaining portion of his lunch break was spent looking out his office window.

He sighed and rubbed his fingers against the streaks of gray encroaching on his temples. Across the street below, children frolicked, screaming while they chased each other and clambered over the playground equipment erected in the park. One young boy sat atop a large rock on the outskirts. His sneakered feet swung back and forth, heels striking the plaque bearing Caleb's name amongst the donors. Each unheard thud against the metal reminded Caleb of the beat of a younger, healthier heart.

How old was I the last time I hung upside down on the monkey bars until I got lightheaded? Or played kickball? Or had any actual fun?

The laughter below dredged Brian's grin from the depths of his memory, a lopsided assortment of gaps and baby teeth. He remembered their mother saving a few of the latter in a family album. Steel and asphalt had claimed the rest. The tombstone tint tainted everything after, blending the years into an opaque sludge. He closed his eyes and tried to sort out the blur.

I've worked here for . . . fifteen years? Is that right? No vacations and just a couple sick days every other year or so? He furrowed his brow, the spot between his eyes itchy. *And how many hours did I work this week? Last week? With all the overtime, I can't even keep track, anymore.*

He opened his eyes and sighed at the stack of files awaiting his attention on the corner of his desk. Satisfying his guilt and nostalgia with a final glance outside, he smiled as he watched a little boy cross the street to join the children gathered on the jungle gym. Several of the kids clambered down when the newcomer bounced an oversized red ball on the ground and back into his hands.

The children formed a circle around the new kid while the ball spun on his finger. The sphere remained perfectly in place even when he made a revolution around it. Caleb did a double take when the kid finally faced him and revealed the sunglasses on his face.

And it's gloomy out right now, too. Is he . . . blind? But then, he doesn't have a cane or a caretaker with him. Maybe he just has a really premature sense of fashion. Caleb chuckled. *Well, hell, good for you either way, kid.*

The group grew, tightening around the boy until Caleb could no longer make him out at all. All he could see were the little ones in back craning their necks to get a better look at whatever trick was being performed for them.

Brian's face emerged from the murk again. The

voice that never got the chance to break reached him in an echo over the whirring spokes of the little bike. The truck's engine wasn't in earshot yet.

"Hey, Caleb! Watch this!"

Caleb cringed while he swept the refuse of his meal into the wastepaper basket resting by his feet. When he looked back out the window, the boy's spot was empty once again. All that remained was the ball left in his stead.

Still spinning . . .

Caleb's fingers twitched, unable to remember what the texture should be like.

Enjoy it while you can, kids. The good stuff never lasts.

It was almost seven o'clock when Caleb finally got up and stretched his back. He'd managed to whittle the mass of paperwork down to a handful of documents. The stray files offended his sense of order, but it was no worse than the picking of an old scab. His finger flipped through the massive stack of finished work.

There's no point being annoyed, anymore. Tight deadlines and overwork are par for the course. Management would never dare give their employees enough time to have a life. Just bonuses and incentives to keep them tied to the job. To tighten that noose.

Reordering the files and locking them in his desk, Caleb went to retrieve his hat and coat from the antique coat rack standing by his window. The rack's placement was no accident. Even vacant, a final look at the haven he'd helped build did his heart some good.

The fall weather brought dusk early. The illumination of the streetlights made glittering shards of the mica trapped in the street. Dull yellow light played over the wooden and plastic structures littering the playground, casting long shadows on the carpet of gravel covering the area. The shapes of seesaws and swing sets took on a sinister appearance after dark, but the haunted house look of the place heartened Caleb rather than disturbed him.

All it takes is a little life to make the place a miniature paradise again. A few laughing voices, some sneaker soles, and a whole lot of energy let loose to just . . . be. Brian would've loved it.

Caleb's vision remained trained on the area below as he pulled the coat over his shoulders. He was about to reach for his hat when a flash of red streaked across the rungs in the jungle gym.

Squinting, Caleb was about to chalk the movement up to distance and a trick of the light when the flicker of scarlet came again. He could have sworn he heard the echo of the rubber as the ball dropped and bounced back into the little hands outstretched from the shadow of the jungle gym.

Caleb slowly placed the hat on his head, trying to process what he was seeing.

What on earth are parents thinking letting their kids stay out so late? Caleb scanned the playground but found no other stragglers. Young or old. *Definitely no parents around. Not even any other kids. So, what's he doing here?*

It was hard to make out details in the darkness, but

Caleb had gotten a decent look at the boy while he was crossing the street. Neither the kid's green T-shirt nor his jeans looked as though they'd had any holes in them. The white sneakers hadn't borne any grass stains. Even the boy's dark hair looked short enough to have been recently cut. The other children hadn't shied away from him, either.

A runaway? The thought turned Caleb's stomach. *It's supposed to downpour tonight. Almost two inches. And there's no cover to speak of down there.*

Caleb finally tore his gaze away long enough to leave his office. His hand toyed with the phone in the pocket of his coat, 9-1-1 only three buttons away. He forced himself to let go of the device.

Whatever the kid's situation is, jumping the gun isn't going to help. For all you know, his parents are just half-assed, or he sneaks out while they work a second shift. The best thing to do right now is to get the story from the horse's mouth.

Stopping at the staff break room on the way downstairs, Caleb rummaged in the fridge. There wasn't much left beyond a ham sandwich wrapped in tinfoil. The Post-It attached read, "Tom."

Sorry, buddy. I'll bring it back safe and sound tomorrow if nobody needs it.

Even so, he left a five-dollar bill in the sandwich's place before rewrapping the food and placing it in the pocket of his coat. Caleb tried not to let the act of minor theft pick at him as he left his building and walked to the edge of the street.

He tried to find the boy again, his toes tapping in his shoe while he waited for the crosswalk's light to change. There was no longer any movement in the shadows. The darkness remained undisturbed even when he was given the chance to cross.

Maybe that boy really was just a straggler, after all . . .

Caleb walked to the spot the boy had occupied by the jungle gym. There was a small crater in the gravel to mark where the ball had repeatedly struck the ground. There was even a faint scent of rubber lingering in the air. However, while there were impressions to mark where the boy had stood, the trail was impossible to follow under the scores of other sneaker impressions left behind. A quick search of the rest of the area yielded no further trace of the boy. When he tried to recall the kid's face, it blended with Brian's behind the black sunglasses. Caleb had to bang his head on the footholds beside him to split the images apart.

He's not *Brian! Not your responsibility. So he was out late. Big deal. There could be a dozen reasons for it. Meanwhile, here's a grown man skulking around a vacant playground after dark. Real smart.*

He grumbled and kicked at the gravel before heading back to the sidewalk.

I just hope nobody saw me. Having some concerned citizen call the cops on me would be the perfect way to cap this fabulous evening.

The annoyance clung to him as he crossed the street and made his way down the shallow slope that led to his office building's garage. Caleb pulled his keys from his pocket, his finger pressing the button on his car alarm while he listened for the beep. He followed the direction of the sound in a huff.

Fifteen years of solid service and I still don't have my own damned parking space.

His footfalls echoed in the space as he went on, the hood of his Chevy finally coming into view. He was no more than a few yards away when the slap of rubber on asphalt interrupted the rhythm of his steps. Caleb flinched in the direction of the sound and saw small hands bathed in shadow. His back resting against one of the pillars, the boy from the playground bounced the ball again.

The kid? From before?

Taking a step closer, Caleb saw the boy was a bit younger than he'd first thought. At only about four feet tall, the child's face was round, his features almost cherubic below the dark hair covering his forehead. Only the sunglasses betrayed the impression. The black lenses looked as if they'd be more at home on an insect. Or a spider.

Caleb stopped when the boy finally acknowledged his presence. He was unsure what to say as the boy clutched the ball to his chest. The words came out more tentative than he'd hoped.

"Um . . . are you okay, kid?"

"Oh, fine." The boy shifted the ball in his arms. The action was gentle—almost loving—as if the toy were some kind of pet. "How about you?"

Caleb was taken aback by the child's nonchalance.

He actually sounds . . . cheerful. And he looks every bit as clean and well fed as he looked from the window earlier.

Caleb kept his voice gentle. "You do know you're not supposed to be here, right? The security guard will be making his rounds soon. Do you have a place to go?"

The boy's high-pitched giggle took on a madman

quality in its echo. Extending an arm, he let the ball roll down his forearm to his hand. "Anywhere. Everywhere." Caleb didn't know why he was tempted to back away when the child leaned farther out beyond the shadow of the pillar. "You seem like a pretty nice guy. Do you want to see a trick?"

Caleb watched the ball fall from the child's outstretched fingertips. Landing lightly in the shadow of the boy's arm, the ball made a few shallow bounces along its length before it began to roll.

Caleb's patience began to ebb, but he kept his tone kindly. "Now look, I'm only trying to help you out here. Do you have a home? A house you live in? A mom and dad?"

The boy's gaze dropped, his attention rapt on the ball as it drew closer to Caleb's feet. He smiled when the orb bumped into the toe of Caleb's right shoe before coming to a stop. The boy's arm, still outstretched, turned over, his fingers clenching into a fist.

"Gotcha."

Caleb was about to ask what the kid was doing when a numbness crept into the soles of his feet.

Wh-what's wrong with . . .

Looking down, he managed to catch one last fleeting glimpse of the ball before it disappeared into the black puddle spreading around his shoes. The shadow of the boy's hand and arm were connected to the darkness, and Caleb could only struggle while the rest of the child's silhouette glided out to strengthen it.

His hands now free, the boy grinned, giggling as Caleb pulled at one of his legs, gasping at the ice-cold grip the tar had on his ankles while he sank an inch into the murk. Caleb was about to scream for help when the darkness below slithered up his legs, its frozen pressure stealing his voice as it wrapped around his waist. It was only when the boy left the dim safety of the pillar and removed the glasses that Caleb could see the deformity beyond. The sockets looked vacant as an open grave. Then, a dull glimmer of light reflected off the jet black orbs within.

God in Heaven. What is he? What the hell is he?

The kid's voice was still jovial, but the pitch changed its character to something more familiar. Each word stabbed an ice pick into Caleb's chest.

"Hey, Caleb! Watch this!"

That's impossible! It sounds like . . . just like . . .

Caleb watched dumbfounded as the boy interlocked his fingers, their union casting the image of a giant spider on the floor of the garage. The beast looked impossibly real, from spiny hairs to mandibles. The shape didn't just move when the boy wiggled his fingers; it walked. Right toward Caleb.

No!

Caleb tried to shrink back from the raised front legs before the boy parted his hands and let the creature dissipate. He clapped, clearly reveling in his own cleverness.

"One more, mister! Just one more! Promise!"

Pressing his palms back together, the tip of the boy's tongue left his mouth, his brow furrowed in concentration. Slowly, the shape of a huge wolf took form on the asphalt below. Caleb could actually see the muscles in the shadow animal's mouth move when its eyeless face looked to him and snarled. Saliva, *real* saliva, dripped from scimitar teeth as it pulled itself free of the ground. The pressure on Caleb's body barely allowed his lungs a wheeze.

"Oh God . . . "

The boy patted the creature on the back. "Good doggy." Black strands of wiry fur smoothed and prickled back up under his touch, caressing the beast before he took another step and hugged the wolf around the neck. Although he whispered in the creature's ear, Caleb was close enough to hear the words.

The kid's voice was once again his own. His words dripped into the creature's ear as sweet as honey. "Who's a good boy?" The boy scratched his pet under the chin. His eyes locked on Caleb. "He's so sad. So old and still so young. Cares so, so much. Do you think we should take him with us?" He smiled when the wolf grunted—excited. Expectant. "I think so, too. After all, we always have room."

The child pulled away, the wolf's body sliding forward under his hand until its lower half joined with the oily shadows stretched across the ground.

"Now, go on and get your treat."

Caleb could only stare while the creature slid toward him, jaws gaping as it rode the dark current to its prize. The wolf loomed too close to see the boy any longer, but as the beast made the final lunge, Caleb heard him singing. There seemed to be other voices there, too. A playground chorus swelled from somewhere in the tiny frame, and for just a moment, Caleb was sure he heard Brian there, as well.

"Ashes, ashes, we all fall down."

JUMP CUTS

ELLEN HARRIS SLEEPWALKED through town. Reflex lifted her feet with the February drifts, the whiteout in her mind even more complete. Her slow pace through the snow on the ground offered up no sound to wake her from the daily trance while her subconscious gorged on winter scenery, storing the skeleton fingers of white trees for future dreams and nightmares.

A truck sped by her, the spraying of snow under its tires breaking the spell chanted by the wind. Ellen wiped the moisture from her face.

Was that ten minutes I've been walking? She squinted in search of a landmark. *Twenty?*

Ellen hid her face deeper inside the collar of her coat and picked up her pace, desperately trying to return to the dead zone in her head. She strained to find the emptiness, but it was too late. The past coughed the dust from its lungs and whispered to her instead. A different void began to creep inside her, and this one didn't offer the comfort of oblivion. She glared at the taillights disappearing in the flakes.

Why'd you have to wake me up?

The fading glow dredged the flash of lipstick. A

smile. A face. Others began to emerge from the haze in which she stored her memories. Ellen squeezed her eyes shut, shaking the tears loose before they had a chance to freeze.

Damn you, damn you, damn you! I don't want to think!

She averted her eyes and forced her way forward, but it was too late. Snatches of conversations decades old reached for her until she clapped her hands over her ears.

Stop! Just stop!

Ellen ran without purpose until a diner's neon sign drew her to the side of the road.

Yes . . . yes. Sleepy warmth. Bad pop music. Anything to drown it.

Ellen took a step through the doorway, unsure, as the bell fixed to the handle tinkled behind her. A middle-aged woman, her gray hair in a bun, walked up to her with a menu. "One, ma'am?"

Ellen hesitated. The heat felt good, but she was painfully aware of the other booths in the dining area. Bits of conversations and bursts of laughter wafted across the room and made her head swim. The ugliness inside her dug in deeper and pulled. She coughed into her hand.

"Ma'am?"

Ellen bit her lip.

You're not getting away. But at least you can suffer in a comfortable seat with a hot drink.

She sighed. "Yes. One."

Ellen followed the hostess to a booth. Seated, the conversations of the other patrons pushed her until she was crammed against the wall. Ellen refused to take off her coat, huddling deeper inside the folds while the words floating around the diner dredged the ones she tried to forget from the depths. Lullabies and the laughter of little children stung her brain. Teenage promises of eternal friendship followed.

Lies. All of them.

A broken promise waited behind her eyelids each time she blinked. Her father slept in his casket, then her mother. A postcard her best friend had sent ten years earlier before disappearing altogether. Birthday cakes and bottles she'd shared with so many, many more who had simply . . . left. Her hands clasped the edge of the table.

Yes, they left. They all left. So screw it. Screw them. Just let it all bleed away. Let the world bleed away . . .

Ellen's hands began to move on their own under the table, mimicking the procedure they underwent at the auto plant. Still, she saw the couples, the families, the friends.

I wonder how long until you all break apart. A chorus of ex-boyfriends rose inside her skull. *"I love you, Ellen."*

"Shut up," she muttered under her breath. "All of you. Just shut the hell up." When she looked up, the waitress stood beside her with a notepad at the ready. If the server had heard anything, she gave no sign as she slid the pencil out from over her ear. Ellen didn't bother waiting for her to ask.

"Coffee. Black."

The waitress didn't smile when her gaze flitted from the order to Ellen's face. "Sure thing, hon. I'll have it right out."

Ellen cringed as the tone stirred something in her brain. A face, a younger face, tore itself free and superimposed its visage over that of the gray-rooted woman seeking out the pot. The name came to her.

Christ, that's Pam! Pam Healey! And she didn't even recognize me!

This time, Ellen made sure to look up and meet the waitress' eyes when she returned to fill her cup. There was no spark. No flash of recognition. Nothing. Ellen's stare remained fixed on the waitress while the black liquid sloshed into her mug.

The waitress fidgeted with her apron. "You okay, ma'am?"

Ellen's voice came out every bit as bitter as the drink. "Yes. Just fine."

The waitress turned and began to walk away. An invisible cord attached to her counterpart in Ellen's memory, pulling it closer and closer to the front of Ellen's mind.

Pam Healey. We met when we were thirteen. Good friends for four years. Had most of the same classes. She liked blue, not pink. Her birthday was on March fourth. I introduced her to her first boyfriend, Mark. She told me she'd write when she went away to college in Georgia, but she only did for a few months. All this, and she can't remember my face. I know it's been years, but good God, she doesn't even know me!

The farther Pam walked, the harder the cord jerked. The strand felt so solid, Ellen could almost see it, thin and silver, trying to tear her insides out. Enraged, Ellen could take no more. The years had been too cruel, drawn on too long. Inwardly, she grabbed hold of the thread and wrenched back.

Pam stopped in midstride, flinching as if stung by some unseen hornet. Looking around for the source of her pain and finding nothing, she began to walk again. Something lingered behind her.

Ellen sat, stunned. A vaporous shape hung in the space occupied a mere moment ago by Pam's skull. A tightly wound bundle of gray coils, the thing uncurled and floated toward the booth, making Ellen's nose tingle at the scent of cigarettes she'd last smoked with Pam behind their school. The wisp snapped across the last half of the distance like an adder, slamming into Ellen's head even as she tried to stand and shove it away. A scream choked in her throat. She felt the thing slither inside her ears before nestling near the front of her brain.

Get it out!

Ellen pushed away from the table. Her fingers pushed through brown bangs to her forehead but found nothing. A child's voice stopped her inspection.

"Mommy, what's wrong with her?"

Ellen found every face in the place aimed at her. Muttering an apology, she fumbled in her purse for a five and let it fall to the table.

Ellen jogged through the door for home, the tickle in her head worsening with every step. She hurried down the streets and finally slammed the door of her apartment shut behind her. Panting, she let her back slide against the portal. Her arms rested on her knees.

What's happening? Am I going nuts? Her hands balled into fists. *All I did was notice Pam, then I felt something and . . .*

A mechanical stutter clattered in her ears as the image of her former friend entered her mind. The pressure in the front of her skull eased while a dull light flickered against the tiles on her kitchen floor. Cloudy at first, forms grew distinct through the haze.

Ellen's eyes bulged further when she saw herself enter the diner. The image went black, a reel missing, as it jumped to Pam tossing in bed, kissing a man beside her before she got up. Spellbound, Ellen watched Pam's life unspool before her. Hours passed. There were friends, children, and a marriage before that. And all the emotions looped back to their source.

So beautiful. So, so beautiful . . .

She clutched her chest, the warmth of each scene entering her, lighting the void she'd nursed for so long. When the scenes reached Pam's college years, the phantom film flickered out and died. Ellen wiped away the tears streaming from her face. The heat inside her was still there, dying embers waiting to be stoked again. Trembling, she licked her lips.

I need more.

Ellen was all too eager to escape work the next day. For the first time, the monotony of her job rankled her, the experiences she'd stolen prodding her and making her hands clumsy. This time, a victim of the cold from her first step outside, she set out for the diner.

Her gaze flitted about the place, but Pam was nowhere in sight. A short twenty-something with a pixie cut brought her to a table instead.

I guess I missed old Pam on a day off. She smiled and giggled to herself. *Not that it matters. I've got everything I want from her already. Let's see what else is in stock . . .*

Ellen scanned the place again. Across the aisle from her, a mother sat with her little boy, about five. Farther away, a couple of teenagers were in some kind of debate while they shoveled pieces of steaming omelets into their mouth. One waitress, a pretty young blonde, flirted with a man sitting alone in his booth.

Ellen swallowed hard.

Remember how it felt before. Even if you don't know these people, the bullshit is always the same. Let it make you just as angry. Let it lead you. Focus . . .

Ellen concentrated on one table at a time. The patrons and their conversations provided mere shadows of people she'd known—fragments—but they slowly dredged the specters of old relationships. Old pains. It wasn't long before she could find a new face for each diner.

Deeper . . .

The cords began to glisten. They were far thinner than the other—almost spider silk—and the pull weak. Yet, the more Ellen discerned the estranged parents, broken friendships, and unfaithful boyfriends, the higher the pressure built.

That's it! Almost!

The force ripped at her and she tore back until a cloudy form freed itself of each and every head. This time, she sat and let them find her, their narrow shapes striking into her like stingers. They roiled inside, fighting for space until they managed to squeeze in beside one another. Ellen smiled, ignoring the nosebleed that followed.

Got you . . .

This time, she sat long enough to enjoy her coffee and receive her check. She tipped big.

Ellen glanced back from the doorway on her way out and looked upon the faces of the strange people who would soon be a part of her. She tried to assuage the pangs of regret and self-loathing that followed her outside.

Don't kid yourself. You know damn well it's the only way they'll stay. Or at least the good parts, anyway.

The stolen memories sat heavy in her head while she again braved the winter weather. She had to step lively to keep the drifts from swallowing her feet as she pulled her coat more tightly around her body, the wind whipping ice and flakes inside her collar. Cold and tired by the time she arrived home, she set to work on a fresh cup of coffee to heat her belly.

Taking a seat on her couch, cup in hand, she focused her eyes on a large, white curtain she'd draped over the television in her living room specifically for the occasion.

All that's left is to start the show.

Thinking back to the faces in the diner, the whirring started in her ears. There was much to see, much to steal, in the images that flowed inside her. Dancing, first kisses, lazy days on beaches, and small feet running wild on the gravel of a playground: It was all there, all hers, and she glutted herself on the beautiful things she knew to be beyond her.

Her soul full, tired, she let the projector in her head continue on, curious to see what else was left on the reel she'd spliced together. She frowned slightly when Pam's experiences took center stage again.

I've had enough of her already. Let's skip to something new . . .

Ellen tried to adjust the picture, but the images remained. And they were not the ones she'd enjoyed the other day.

The important parts of the college years played out in their entirety, a jump cut marking the end of each sequence as the film played in reverse. Abruptly, Ellen's high school appeared on her makeshift screen. Her teenage face stared back at her, a smile already souring just slightly at the edges cutting her mouth. The frame got stuck in the reel. When it came free, the film lurched forward rather than back. She was in all of it. The cup fell from her hand and shattered on the floor.

No . . . stop . . .

She watched the bags under her eyes darken and spread like fresh bruises, her smile growing tighter and her eyes duller with each progressive scene. It reminded her of a time-lapse clip show of a decomposition. Ellen was ill by the time the next gap came and returned her again to the diner. Her face, lost, weathered, and vicious, glared back at her from the booth. The ugliness of it had been too familiar to notice earlier. Now, it was unbearable.

That's enough!

Ellen lunged across the room and tore the curtain loose before the film could sputter out. The only image left in her mind was that of her own reflection. She raced outside, the visage picking at her as her feet sank into the snow. The reel continued spinning between her eyes.

Stop! Please, for the love of God, stop!

She finally stumbled and fell, drowning up to her waist in one of the mounds shoveled beside the road. She fought to free herself while the projector continued its show. Cold inside and out numbed her into submission as she felt the loss sink into her heart and learned that not all of it belonged to her.

THE SKIN TRADE

CARL HANSON NURSED his whiskey and soda at the hotel bar. He observed the man reflected in the polished wood under his elbows, his free hand unsure whether to smooth the streak of gray hair resting near his temple or hide it. Carl grimaced, sharpening all the little lines in his face he was learning to hate. The smooth, hungry faces of the others he'd met at the conference leered through his memory.

Young Turks as far as the eye can see. Probably snickering behind my back as soon as I got off stage. Or just planning how to gun for me. Well, I may be getting a little gray and overweight, but I'm not dead yet, kiddies.

Carl downed the rest of his drink. Setting the glass down, his eyebrows raised when the bartender gave him a refill without prompting.

The young man looked at Carl over his shoulder while returning the bottle to its spot on the shelf. White teeth flashed a conspiratorial smile in his tan face.

"Courtesy of the lady at the end of the bar, sir."

Carl leaned back on his stool to glance around the other patrons. A lovely face grinned back at him. A woman in her late twenties with lipstick as scarlet as her dress and the curls in her hair. Carl felt his face blush the same color and offered a clumsy smile back.

See that, boys? I told you I'm not dead!

Straightening his suit, he rose and approached the empty seat beside the lady with his drink in hand. Long, elegant fingers patted the cushion before he could sit down. The scent of lilacs wafted to him when she turned green eyes on him that shamed the luster of the nearby bottles. A bemused smile played on her lips while he struggled for something to say. And even when she finally broke the silence for him.

"You're a quiet one, aren't you?"

Carl tried to hide the pleasant shiver that ran through him at the husky tone of her voice.

"I suppose I am." He chuckled, lifting his whiskey. "Thank you, though. For the drink."

She grinned, every tooth perfectly in line. "You're very welcome. So, are you here on business or pleasure?"

Carl sipped at his drink. "Business. A conference, actually. Terribly routine stuff." He managed a shy smile over the lip of the glass. "Pleasant company aside, of course."

"I'm flattered." She slid a few inches closer to him, the floral scent—or extra liquor—now strong enough to give him a buzz. "How long are you going to be in town, Mr . . . ?"

"Hanson. Carl Hanson." He tried to shake off an internal groan at what had sounded like a bad Bond impersonation. "Only until tomorrow evening, I'm afraid. The flight back to Phoenix is at six. And you are?"

"Layla."

He barely got the next sip down when he felt the gentle pressure of her hand on his. The buzz in his head jumped to another level at the contact, the pumping of his heart suddenly a distinct sensation in his chest.

"A lot can happen in 24 hours, Carl. Would you mind if I show you?"

Carl fumbled for his wallet, leaving a generous tip before standing to extend his arm. "It would be my pleasure."

She giggled softly before slipping beside him. "Such a gentleman."

Despite the drink, Carl felt himself standing straighter than he had the entire weekend. His mood became almost giddy when he noticed a small group of the young businessmen he'd encountered earlier on the way out. He rewarded the double takes with a wink.

Let that *image stick in your craws on the flight home.*

Carl felt like he was walking in a dream on the way up the stairs. His entire body felt so light that it might just float the rest of the way up on its own. Even so, ugly little doubts picked at the back of his head.

What is it they say about things that are too good to be true? Do you remember? What if she's got somebody waiting up there to cold cock you and take your wallet? What if she's a call girl?

Carl looked at the woman in his arms. The delicious heat of her body pressed against his only made the fog filling him thicken.

Then, I'll pay. God help me, I'll pay . . .

Now in the hall of rooms upstairs, he started moving toward his room until Layla placed a hand against his chest. She steered him to the left with a giggle.

"I'm in Room 203, silly."

He drifted with her to the door of her room, feeling as though he might melt into her while she slid the key card. The feeling intensified when she pulled him inside and closed the door. In the darkness, Carl felt her lips press against his own. The lilac aroma filled his senses to the brim, seeming to thin the air itself until everything went black.

The euphoria peaked, then ebbed while her hands ran over his body. Her fingertips seemed to seek out the deepest lines in his face, moving to touch gray streaks in his hair she shouldn't be able to see. They even wandered down to the slight gut he'd built over the last few years. He shivered, suddenly aware of just what a ridiculous mismatch they were—how far he'd fallen from his prime.

He held her closer, his mouth forming words he couldn't hear through the mist still filling his head. Layla's examination became more soothing while he spoke, building the lightness inside him to a new level until it drowned his consciousness under cotton.

Carl awoke to the same darkness. Stifling hot, he tried to throw the sheets off him. His arms didn't move.

Man, I must've really overdone it last night.

Carl tried again. Panic began seeping in when he

met the same resistance. He felt rested, but there was no light. No sun.

Layla . . .

He tried to speak her name but all that escaped was air. It mingled with the humid atmosphere surrounding him, making it even harder to breathe. The sweat coming off him didn't feel as if it were soaking any bedding. Instead, it seemed as though it were pooling over him. Basting him.

Carl fought with his body to find it a numb limb. It took all his concentration just to lift his head a fraction of an inch. When he did, it pressed against something with the texture of wet vinyl. The jolt of adrenaline that followed let his fingertips inch out to find the same material waiting there, as well.

Fuck! What did she do to me? Where am I?

Visions of a squirming form inside a body bag dragged Carl's fingernails against the barrier. His breathing became more ragged, further deepening the heat. Eating up the air.

I need to get out. I have to get out!

He struggled, trying to find any purchase to attack the thing holding him. Wriggling degenerated to a full-body clench that rolled him to his side. His face mashed against the material so hard he could taste it. Moist, rotten sweet, and salty, the flavor made him gag out most of his remaining air. Lungs scorched, he bit into the stuff and pulled.

A wet tearing sound reverberated in the tiny space. Daylight and chilled air rushed in through the hole, revitalizing Carl's system. His teeth ripped the hole wider. Slowly, he forced his head through the opening and saw the carpet below.

Close . . . so close. Just a little more . . .

Gritting his teeth, Carl wriggled forward. His shoulders pushed and stretched the gap until they popped free, dragging the rest of his squirming body out until he struck the floor.

Carl crawled to the wall and pushed himself up to his feet. Bile rose in his throat again when he looked upon the trail of fluid leading from the human shape resting on the bed. Pale as the moon, it continued to leak like a squashed bug; it smelled even worse.

Carl stumbled forward, extending a shaking hand to touch a prison he'd only expected to escape in death. Lines and scars he'd known for a lifetime rested on its surface. Even the hairs remained. Between gray temples, the remains of Carl's old face gaped at him broken-jawed—an eyeless, toothless mask. He backed away.

Fuck. Oh, fuck me. What did she . . . Where is . . . ?

Carl scanned the room, but Layla hadn't left so much as an impression on the bed. Checking the bathroom, he found his own toothbrush and razor on the sink. The sight was still processing when he saw himself in the mirror. His hands wandered over the new flesh, all of it simultaneously alien and familiar.

Everything looks *the same . . .* He pinched the layer of fat over his stomach. *Feels the same. Am I . . . okay?*

Carl backed out of the room and checked the closet. His luggage and clothes waited inside.

This is my room. She dragged me back here somehow.

He glanced behind him at the skin resting on the bed. The new skin proved it could crawl as well as the old.

My room . . . I can't let anybody find this thing here! If the maid comes in and finds this thing, there's going to be a SWAT team waiting for me at the airport.

Carl's gaze fell back to his luggage. He grimaced at the thought of the skin touching his clothes, hefting its weight.

No choice. Just . . . do it. Fast.

Setting his jaw, Carl stalked back to the bed and lifted the remains. The liquid inside had dried at an unnatural rate. There was barely even a stain on the carpet where the majority of the stuff had slopped. Nonetheless, the texture of the skin made him queasy. He rolled the flesh up as best he could and crammed it in the suitcase, crushing it down with his clothes.

After packing the rest of his things, Carl toweled off and put on the one suit he'd left out. Straightening the knot on his tie, he took a deep breath and headed out the door.

Maintaining a casual air proved impossible. The heat and sensation of cell-produced vinyl was still superglued to his flesh. And Carl could've sworn there was a trace of lilac perfume escaping through the suitcase. It took him a moment to realize it was wafting from the open door to Layla's room. He jumped back when a vacuum roared to life inside. Peering in, he waved at the middle-aged maid inside until she switched the machine off.

"Uh, excuse me, miss. The lady staying here— would you happen to know if she checked out?"

She put a palm to the small of her back and stretched. "She left about half an hour ago, I think. Was she a friend of yours or something?"

Carl replied with a tight smile and shake of his head before heading down the stairs, the scent following him. Reminding him. He was nauseous from it by the time he reached the desk.

There was not the barest hint of a smile when he paid the hotel clerk. He could not even manage a "thank you" as the sweat forced his anxious fingers to creep farther down the handle for want of a better grip. Even with the thing inside, the suitcase wasn't heavy, but Carl felt like he was holding a dirty bomb in his hand. His stomach churned while he imagined the case slipping free and breaking open on the ground. The moment of silence, then the screams that would follow.

And most of them would be mine . . .

Carl could almost hear the thing laughing at him inside the suitcase. The ragged flaps of skin that were its mouth fluttered as it chuckled in his voice—from *his* lips. Or what was left of them, anyway.

Carl finally realized the desk clerk was staring and shook his mind free.

There's no time to dwell on things. You've got a human skin—your skin—stuffed in a suitcase like some kind of serial killer. Nobody's going to believe what happened, and you can't put it back on. You have to ditch it.

Doubts still plagued him when he passed through the door. His thumb massaged the suitcase's handle.

Are the prints there still the same? My retinas? My DNA? His grip tightened at the thought of Layla's touch. *Too bad there's only one person who could tell me for sure. And God only knows where she went, the bitch.*

Carl fancied he heard flesh sliding against the leather as he wound his way to the back of the building and behind the Chinese restaurant across the street. Grateful for the dim morning light, Carl took a final look around, removed his skin, and pitched it in the far corner of the receptacle.

He was surprised by how much emotion followed—how much guilt. A sense that he'd just lost something terribly important gnawed at him, as did the feeling that this new flesh might hide a corruption invisible to the naked eye. Carl shook his head.

Stop. You did what you had to. Maybe—maybe it's not even really your skin! Maybe she poured some kind of goop on you that just made an impression. Like some kind of mold or something! Yeah . . . that's it. That's got to be it . . .

The assertion didn't hold back the dry heaves when a length of the skin unfolded beside some pork fat. For a moment, Carl was tempted to rescue the thing, to throw it back into his suitcase and risk the airport scanners.

Yeah, and do what with it? Wear it as a cape? Have a plastic surgeon graft it back on? Don't be stupid, man! Go!

Still, Carl found himself stealing looks back over his shoulder while he made the walk back to the hotel and searched the parking lot. The impulse followed him into his rental car, and he nearly rear-ended someone at the exit while fixing his gaze on the rearview mirror. He was startled less by the sudden pressure instinct forced on the pedal than by the streak of red rushing past him down the street.

Layla.

Carl didn't understand how he knew it was her. It was only a second—less than a second—that he had glimpsed the driver through her window, but his body moved of its own accord. He barely heard the horn of the car in front of him before he swerved around it onto the grass and gave chase.

As the miles passed, Carl became increasingly sure the woman knew she was being tailed. She seemed to slow and yield for a car whenever he started to fall too far back, and to make sure he was only a few car lengths behind before making a turn. Once, he thought he even caught her peering at him from her side-view mirror. He could have sworn she was smiling.

Oh, don't worry, bitch. I'm coming for you! Carl's hands tightened around the wheel. *And what are you going to do when you catch her? What is* she *going to do when you catch her?* His fingernails bit the plastic, the digits less weathered than they were supposed to be. *Damn it, I have to know . . .*

The woman's car eventually slowed to a crawl and parked beside the strangest-looking apartment building Carl had ever seen. Whatever residual confidence he'd had was gone, as was his stamina, but the building did wonders for his fears. Layla was already up the steps and inside by the time Carl wobbled his way out of the car.

He could not say what aspect of the place disturbed him most. Part of it was surely the paint job. A horrible kaleidoscope of yellow and black was splotched all over the façade. If there was a pattern to the design, he could not find it, and yet, he somehow knew it was there, nonetheless. The building also seemed strangely asymmetric, off-center, and even looking at it strained his eyes. He could almost see the place bending in the wind as if it were some gigantic plant. His nose wrinkled at the floral smell wafting to him from the place.

"It even smells like her . . . "

Carl flinched when he finally noticed the face watching him from a window near the entrance. He moved forward at the exact same instant the visage disappeared, prompting him to give chase yet again. He had little time to register either the aura of strangeness he penetrated upon entering or the dust floating through the air. It was the flash of ankle at the top of the stairway he noticed, then a wisp of crimson trailing behind a corner as he pushed himself up the steps.

By the time he reached the fifth floor, Carl was sorely wishing she'd just used the elevator. His clothes were soaked through, and there was an awful buzzing in his ears to go with the lactic acid scorching his side. However, there was nowhere else to climb.

He meant to look menacing when he rounded the corner into the building's topmost and furthest corridor. Layla was not far enough ahead to hide the movement of a door or the latching of a deadbolt.

She's close. And there's only one door open.

Carl didn't understand why the snarl left his face the moment he passed the threshold, or why the cramp in his stomach seemed to loosen when Layla turned to face him. Perhaps it was the way she looked at him, or the sound of her voice. There was no fear there—only love. Carl found himself too weak to push her away when she trotted forward and threw her arms around his neck.

"I'm so glad you kept up, Carl! I'm sorry I had to be so evasive, but I doubt you would have followed me here any other way. How are you feeling?"

Carl was glad his voice still had some anger left. The rest of him felt too much like jelly to rage. That, and she felt so comfortable against him. She was so cool she almost burned.

"What the hell did you do to me last night?"

Layla gave him a coy tilt of her head. "Do?"

Carl grabbed her arms and lifted her to her toes. "I almost choked to death on my own skin this morning! I ended up shedding the whole thing like a damned snake! Now, what did you *do!?*"

Layla's laughter was cheerful even after he pushed her away. The sound was like the echo of wet crystal. The noise rippled through his body and mingled with the ringing in his ears. "I did what you told me to, silly! Don't you remember what we discussed?"

"What the hell are you talking about?"

At this, a pout crossed her lips before they lifted into another smile. "I keep forgetting how drowsy you were. It was right before you drifted off that you said it."

"Oh, for fuck's sake! Said what?"

Layla leaned forward slightly. Her voice was soft as feathers as it left her lips. "'What do you want with an ugly old bastard like me?' Your words, not mine."

Carl felt a rush of blood in his clammy cheeks. "I . . . what?" Carl said, shaking his head. "I make over six digits a year! I make careers, and I break them! And on top of that, I don't look any worse than the next guy on the street!"

Her voice lilted. It was almost singing. "Very ugly,

Mr. Hanson, and yet so very vain." She laughed again when he reached out to slap her only to find his hand a good two feet off target. It was as if she had danced out of the way—or floated. "But that's all in the past," she said. "You wished for beauty. You wished it of me, through me, and you did so honestly. How could I deny you? Just look at you, poor dear!"

Again, she swayed out of Carl's reach. This time, he tripped. A wild grab caught a nearby windowsill and left him face-to-face with his reflection.

He strangled a sob. He remembered.

It was all there, precisely as before. The gray roots peering through the dye, the slight jowls, and the angry little lines beside his mouth and eyes all remained. He was a pig masquerading as a man. Only the suit looked good.

Nothing's changed at all . . .

Layla flitted closer, her voice still music. "You begged me, Carl. And now, you shall have your wish."

This time, he did not draw away when her arms encircled him, nor did he so much as flinch as every hair below his neck stretched and tensed into wire-like rigidity. The itch of a thousand crawling ants erupted along his shoulder blades. He struggled, trying to scratch away the pain, but Layla held him fast. Seconds later, there was a tearing of cloth as wings unfolded—black and yellow—from his back. Layla snuggled closer with a grin, her dress peeling off her with a sound like falling silk. Red wings fluttered behind her before they slowed, flexing in time with his own.

She stroked his cheek, "Shh, my love. Rest. Things will look better in the morning."

Again, Carl felt drunk and tired. He did not fight

when his lover helped him to the floor. As his eyes closed, he wondered what would be waiting in the mirror when he awoke.

THE DECONSTRUCTIONIST

ANDY HARPER DRANK in the world he'd wrought. The spires of massive skyscrapers pierced the clouds and gouged the ionosphere. Far below, the tangle of glass and steel stretched across the landscape. The streets that had once connected the buildings were no longer necessary. The roads had simply been swallowed up as the structures grew, the bulk of each tower melting into the next until all were united. Vacant, the rows of buildings stood sentry over what few patches of bare space remained below. All was silent until Andy's mutter of disgust.

It's gone stale? Already?

He waved his hand and let it all dissolve. As the structures had been built, they vanished, their outlines shimmering while the molecules composing them lost their solidity and came apart. Dozens of miles of metropolis were reduced to a vacant lot in a matter of seconds. Only a few places that held the essentials of life were allowed to remain behind. Andy sat and rested his narrow chin on his knuckles. His friend, Gerry, tittered nervously beside him.

"That was awful fast, Andy. Is there something new you want to try out?"

Andy scratched his neck with his thumb. "No . . . not yet. I just got sick of looking at it, y'know?"

Gerry patted him on the shoulder, the expression on his round, bespectacled face accommodating as always. "That's okay. You'll think of something. You always do."

"Yeah . . . sure."

Andy sighed and looked upon the newly minted wasteland.

Maybe I should try to put the Army back together. Those tanks and planes were pretty fun to mess with. They'd probably bring even more stuff to see if I let them in again.

Andy looked to the horizon and squinted. The wall that had been built around his hometown was little more than a pencil line in the distance. He grunted and scratched the idea.

Nah. Those guns and bombs gave me a headache after the first day. Freaked Gerry out, too. Besides, beating them was so easy. Doing it again would be so . . . boring.

Andy stretched an arm over his head and let photographic memory replay the evolution he'd brought about—the hundreds of cities he'd created over the ruins of the old. The architecture had run the gamut from art deco to Islamic temple, Escher monstrosity to Roman splendor, before he'd started merging them into new shapes altogether. His mind skimmed the remnants of countless TV shows, websites, and magazines for fresh inspiration.

Maybe some of those New England slanty roofs? No . . . done it already. Or maybe . . . Ugh! Too close to that one I tried a few months ago. Andy rubbed his temples, a vein in his forehead starting to throb. *When did this start getting so hard?*

His left leg asleep, Andy got up and tried to rub the numbness away. Launching a wad of phlegm in the wasteland's direction, he started out on a walk, his eyes hunting for a fresh muse. Gerry followed close behind, panting as his chubby legs struggled to keep up. Andy smiled at his friend's wheezing.

Good old Gerry. He never complains. Not when the bullies beat him up for sticking up for me and not when he hid the bruises he showed up with at the bus stop.

Andy hocked another loogie in the general direction of the middle school.

All those people and the only one of them worth keeping around is a fat ginger kid with asthma who sweats when he eats. But you never ask me to fix any of it for you, do you, Ger? You just tough it out every time. And smile.

Andy heard Gerry swallow, clearing his throat before he spoke. "Where are we going, Andy?"

He shrugged. "I don't know. Just walking. Maybe we'll go back to the library later."

Andy fidgeted, remembering just how many travel books were already cracked open and piled up on the table. His mood continued to darken the farther they walked. Memory assured him that every idea that came to him was one he had acted on before.

What's wrong with me? It's only been a year since I took this place. I shouldn't be burned out yet. So, how come after all I've done, I still don't like this stupid place any better than I did before?

Andy slowed his pace when he came to the base of

a hill. The wheezing behind him had worsened. He waited until Gerry's breathing evened out before making the climb. The rise wasn't too high, only about thirty feet or so, but it was enough to view a large chunk of the treeless expanse below. A dull autumn sun tried to paint the dirt and gravel a more cheerful shade and failed. Pebbles a foot or so away from Andy's feet tumbled down while a spate of fresh huffs assured him that Gerry had made it up. Andy waited until the redness left his friend's face before bothering to speak. "Do you ever miss it?" he said. "The way it was, I mean."

Gerry's lips tightened as he pondered the question, his deep-set eyes pulling a bit further back into his head. "Sometimes. There were places I liked. The movie theater was cool, and I liked that ice cream place on the corner of Main Street. I kind of miss my video games, too."

"What about overall? Do you think this is better?"

"Not yet," Gerry said. "But it could be."

Andy grinned and shook his head.

You really couldn't try to bullshit me if your life depended on it, could you?

He motioned forward with a chuckle. "Come on. Let's go to the library."

Andy was glad he'd let the place stand. The stone lions guarding the front stairs were almost life-size versions of the real thing. Their gaze was attentive rather than fearsome while they watched the library's only remaining patrons enter the red brick edifice.

Gerry nearly hacked up a lung when the door opened, but Andy didn't mind the dust. The old pages lent the air and the little clouds formed by the falling particles a vanilla scent. It was like entering a haunted house where all the spirits were friendly. A hint of nostalgia jabbed him as he passed the sections covering reference, folklore, and religion. His memory played back fevered hours spent searching the tomes before giving up on ever finding an explanation for what he was or what he could do. Gerry's inhaler hissed behind him when he reached the travel section and pulled a few fresh books from the shelves.

There's got to be something here. Anything . . .

Andy's eyes flitted over the pages, his mind storing each image and description for further reference.

These ruins at Angkor Thom are kind of cool. Or maybe those old rocks standing in England?

Still, the more he searched, the more he felt something was missing. His rapid flipping through the pages slowed to a crawl before a peculiar noise stopped it altogether. Off to the side, Gerry was stifling a yawn.

I can't believe it. He's bored. Gerry's bored. Andy grimaced and slammed the book in his hands shut. *This . . . isn't fun, anymore. It's boring. It's . . .* empty.

Gerry looked up from the volume he'd been perusing. "What's wrong? No good?"

Andy hung his head. "No. No good at all. I don't get it. I *wanted* to come here, and now that I am, it feels like it's got no point, you know?"

Gerry's face scrunched up, deep in thought again. "Well, you never like doing the same stuff twice. Maybe just doing the city over and over is getting boring, too. Even though you make it different each time, it's still doing the same thing."

Andy paused and thought about his friend's words, his brow furrowing.

He's right—I'm right—but there's something else missing, too. I hated this place so much. Hated the people who hassled us and called me a freak and a witch and beat Gerry up just because they could. Guilt and rage coaxed a shiver at the thought of screams and tangled limbs. Even his powers couldn't make them anything but hideous. *I still want to make it better, just for us. So why doesn't it feel right, anymore?*

He looked at Gerry, remembering all the black eyes and busted lips, the bruises half obscured by the sleeves and collar of his shirt from where his mom hit him. Ones he'd seen so often in the mirror.

All that mean and stupid is just outside. Overflowing. No matter what I build or how long I live, it's going to rush in and eat everything up the second I'm gone.

Andy got up and left the table, shaking, the closed book finally tumbling from his fingers. He felt dizzy, ill. When Gerry asked him what was wrong, his friend sounded as though he were underwater.

Andy took a moment to steady himself on the table's edge. "Come on. Just . . . come on."

He could hardly even see the door. The images of all his previous efforts, his failures, were flashing through his mind. They haunted him as he hurried to the center of the desolation, his head low. He hadn't even realized he'd outpaced Gerry. He watched his friend jog awkwardly to his side.

"Sorry, Ger. Guess I was daydreaming."

Gerry panted, his hands on his knees. "S'okay, man. Just. Wait. A sec."

Andy stretched out his arms. "Don't worry. We're right where we should be."

Gerry looked around, the confusion on his features obvious despite the red tint of his skin. Although the air was cold, sweat had plastered his curly red hair to his forehead.

"I don't get it, Andy. Why are we here?"

Andy knelt and placed a palm on the ground. He smiled as he lifted a handful of dirt and let it pour out between his fingers.

"Because I'm tired of walking and this is as close to the center of this place as I'm going to get." He laughed, picking up another fistful of grit and throwing it into the air. Tears squeezed from his eyes when it landed on his head. "Don't you get it, Ger? No matter what I do, what I build, somebody's going to come around and screw it up. And even if I block it from the whole world, there'll be nobody left to enjoy it when we're gone." He extended his index finger and pointed straight into the air. "But I figured out a way around it."

The scarlet tint drained from Gerry's face. He looked even more pale than usual, but he didn't sound frightened. "So, what do we do?"

"The only thing we can do. We make better people."

This time, Andy did see his friend wince. The ghastly forms of their tormentors twisted in his mind anew.

"No, no," Andy said, shaking the dirt from his head. "Not like that." He grinned, shivering when the first tremors of pain hit his nerves. "This time, I'm going to do it from scratch." He doubled over as the breakdown of his body took hold.

Gerry started toward him. He stumbled when the ground below began to shake. In the distance, a massive sheet of shimmering gas rose like a wall, reaching over the city.

"Andy! I don't understand! What are you doing?"

Andy did his best to speak despite the degeneration of his cells. Everything from his eyes to ankles hurt. "I always really sucked at biology. At chemistry. But there is something I do remember. Something . . . simple." He reached forward and grabbed Gerry's hand. "You can leave whenever you want, but you won't be able to come back in. Nobody will. See ya, Ger."

Andy could feel his body slipping away, liquefying, as it began to squelch inside his clothes. Gerry pulled away while flesh reduced to bacteria and proteins.

Primordial soup, just like the teacher said. The building blocks of life. A better world. Better people . . .

Before his consciousness disappeared completely, Andy saw the tears streaming down the face of the only person brave enough to give a damn about him. With his last act of strength, he resurrected an ice cream shop at the corner of Main Street, its power on and all the flavors cold.

THE LAST GREAT EFFECT

CLYDE REYNOLDS PUSHED his foot down on the accelerator so hard his knee began to ache. He gritted his teeth, dodging around traffic and ignoring the profanity aimed his way through open windows. Reggie's voice again drifted into the car via Bluetooth.

"Clyde? You still there, man?"

Clyde winced as yet another horn blared behind him. "Yeah! Yeah, I'm here. You just stay with me, okay? Just keep talking."

A sigh blew through the speakers. Tired. Dreamy. Clyde cringed deeper into his seat, feeling as if a precursor to his friend's death rattle were blowing into the car like a dry Autumn breeze.

"I've had an awful lot of pills. An awful lot. I'm sorry about all this."

Oh Christ!

Clyde held his breath and blew past a red light. His hands throttled the wheel when the sign for Reggie's street came into view. The car nearly tipped when he spun into the turn.

Almost there. Keep him talking.

"It's okay! I'm your friend, remember? It's been

that way for thirty years. And we're going to do another thirty until we have heart attacks speeding around on set in wheelchairs, you hear me?"

The slightest whisper of a laugh drifted into the car, but it soon faded. Exhaustion and a profound sorrow coated the words that followed.

"I don't think so, Clyde . . . I've got no family, no work. I'm a dinosaur. And it's time I go extinct."

"Reggie? *Reg!*"

Clyde pulled into the driveway so fast he nearly hit the garage. He barely had breath to call in to 9-1-1 before racing out and up the steps to the front door. The knob didn't budge.

Clyde put his shoulder to the door once, damn near breaking the joint before remembering the key in the fake rock beside the steps. His shaking fingers wrestled the key into its hole before he burst inside. Disturbed by the force of the door, dozens of unopened letters slid across the dingy floor.

"Reggie! I'm here! Where are you?"

The tight confines didn't allow the call space to echo. Clyde took in the squalor around him while he searched room to room, shocked at the mess. Empty liquor bottles and the occasional prescription lay scattered about; a thin layer of dust coated the furniture. The only thing that looked cared for was the assortment of special effects relics Reggie had crafted for the studios over the years.

In perfect working order. As always.

A hint of a smile struggled at Clyde's lips when he noticed the motley crew they'd assembled had their own special section around the staircase. A hook-nosed goblin, a trio of dripping mutants, and a winged demon that could've brushed the ceiling were just a few members of the honor guard around the staircase.

Clyde paused by the goblin grinning where it stooped at the foot of the stairs. He could've sworn its gaze was following him up, each creak under his feet doubling for its laughter. There were only two doors at the top. The one to the bedroom hung open. As he drew closer to the gap, Clyde saw a form spread eagle on the bed.

"R-Reg? Oh God. What did you do to yourself?"

His friend's watery blue eyes stared up at him above purple lips. A thick layer of stubble rested on a face that had been kept baby smooth for decades, his normally quaffed hair equally unkempt. Two empty containers of pills stood on his nightstand. Clyde's hand found Reggie's wrist. The flesh there was still warm, but there was no pulse.

"Goddamnit!"

Clyde slammed his foot into the bedpost. The numbness creeping up his leg echoed that of long hours spent working behind the scenes, Reggie always smiling despite the blisters. His hands that had mended metal and wire like a master pianist whenever help was needed. The gentle voice that never failed to find something soothing to say even when a budget was slashed or a heart got broken off set. Tears were already burning Clyde's eyes when he noticed the folded collection of papers falling to the floor from where it had been camouflaged by the bed sheets. He knelt, unsure whether to read the note or not just as the sirens wailed into earshot. He steeled himself.

You owe him that much.

Unfolding the note, Clyde began to read. He

blinked through the tears, shocked into a stupor at the thoughts his friend had detailed so clearly on the pages. Clyde was still shaking his head, saltwater dampening the papers when the paramedics stormed upstairs.

Clyde pocketed the note, operating on autopilot while the men made their examination and asked their questions. He didn't even comprehend his own words. There were only the ones repeating in his head—the first step of the task he was to do.

I need to make some calls.

Clyde added another empty shot glass to the growing pyramid on the bar. Beside him, director Manny Vasquez looked through the pages of Reggie's suicide note for a third time. His first drink remained forgotten by his elbow, his pudgy face inscrutable save for a slight pallor clinging to the tan skin.

Clyde tapped the apex of the pyramid loud enough to make his friend drop the pages on the bar.

"The words don't change, Manny. I need to know. Are you with me on this or not?"

Manny scratched at the thick black beard covering his cheeks. The quiver in his voice rippled his stomach like a Jell-O mold. However, there was no mistaking the excitement underneath.

"The logistics of this are insane. You know that, right? Preposterous."

Clyde smiled and motioned the bartender for another shot. "Of course. But you'll do it, anyway, won't you?"

Manny finally slipped his fingers around his glass and took a sip of rum.

"Reggie was my idol since I was a kid. I studied every movie he worked on growing up. I even tried to replicate some of the practicals myself in my garage once I knew how they worked. And his effects are as much a part of the first movies I did as I am. He gave me my start in every way." He downed the rest of the shot in one deep gulp. "So, fuck yes. Count me in. And meet me at my studio at six."

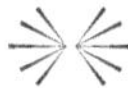

Clyde squirmed in the pew. The assortment of veils and black suits dredged up unpleasant memories. Old nightmares.

I still remember Uncle Joe's funeral back when I was five. And that damn clown makeup they spackled on him.

A twinge of nausea entered Clyde's stomach when he flashed back to the closed eyes snapping open to reveal gaping sockets infested with worms. He looked from the casket to the wrinkles webbing his own hands and made a fist.

Pain pulsed along his back as he resisted the urge to stretch his spine over the back of the pew. He was easily the oldest man at the tinsel town service, complete with gray hair, wrinkles, and a pair of glasses thicker than most of the phones lighting the area. He shook his head.

And Reggie was a year younger, wasn't he?

Had Clyde indulged in hair dye and a facelift, the side of the aisle he occupied would still have given him away. There were no more than a dozen men seated in his half of the church, all of them middle-aged to elderly. The other was packed with fresh Hollywood faces obscured behind dark sunglasses.

I wonder how many of them even know who he was beyond the obituary and that "legend" status of his. I'm sure they think it's a great photo op, though—showing some respect for the old guard. Not that they ever gave him any while he was alive. After all, they had appointments with plastic surgeons and drug dealers to attend.

Clyde's fingers cramped while his hands tightened their grip around his knees. He caught a few young faces looking his way before they noticed they'd been spotted and returned their attention to the reverend's service. Clyde's roving gaze noted more than one CG studio head in the crowd—and plenty of directors who adored them. His lips twisted into a sneer.

It takes a special kind of gall to attend the funeral of a man you murdered. I watched you loop the rope around his neck, tightening it for years before kicking the chair out from under him. And for what? Garbage. Pure and utter garbage.

Clyde flashed back to the last outing he'd had with Reggie. Their annual trip to the movies in honor of their first collaboration. Reggie had always been dapper—handsome and well-kept. This time, his suit had been rumpled and the tie on crooked. His hair, always short, was in dire need of a trim, though not as badly as it had been on the bed. Cologne couldn't hide the whiff of vodka clinging to his clothes. They said little to each other beyond pleasantries before the film started.

THE LAST GREAT EFFECT

The movie was sub B-level "sci-fi" garbage, rampant with bad writing and computer-generated effects at center stage. Clyde's expression went sour after fifteen minutes. No prosthetics. No decent makeup work. No animatronics. No nothing. He didn't understand how anyone could feel wonder at the spectacle when its origin, its magic, was so painfully obvious.

He'd looked to Reggie to exchange a jibe only to find his friend's eyes hollow. Reggie had turned to him, his expression pained and his voice carrying all the emotion the picture lacked. "You can't fight progress, buddy." The words stabbed Clyde in the gut again.

He used to say the same thing to rally the crew when they were behind schedule or struggling with a job. Now, it just sounds like an epitaph.

Clyde's fingernails bit into the fabric covering his knees. He was glad no one was close enough to see the small scarlet circles that blossomed on his pants. The waste of life and talent left him ill, as did the blank expressions of the mourners. Aside from those on his side, they knew nothing of what they were missing.

And it's our duty to change that. My duty.

Even though Clyde had been waiting for the tap on his shoulder, the contact made him flinch. Manny squeezed in next to him. Clyde couldn't imagine how such a large man had slipped into the church without making a sound. Manny leaned in close enough to ensure not a syllable could be overheard. Clyde almost expected the wiry beard hairs to prick his cheek when Manny spoke in his ear.

"We're ready."

Clyde smiled at him and nodded. "Thanks. For everything."

A ghost of a chuckle escaped Manny's lips, but the words were solemn. Reverent. "Anything for Reggie." He checked his watch, his voice suddenly apprehensive as the second hand ticked down. "Five. Four. Three . . ."

Action.

The reverend was right where they wanted him. He'd just ended the service, the pipes of the organ filling the church with their dirge. The pall bearers were still en route to the coffin when its door swung open. Reggie sat up and turned his glassy eyed gaze on the mourners. The skin on his face twitched as the workings underneath stirred to life and tugged at wires. Slowly, his lips stretched into a grin.

Clyde wasn't sure if he coughed out a bark of laughter or a sob. The young Hollywood crowd on the other side of the aisle went into a panic, the terror in their eyes clear when the dark glasses dangled from one ear or fell to the floor. The quarters were too cramped to easily escape the pews. Few managed to get to the doors before Reggie was on his feet. Clyde glanced from his friend to the tiny remote engulfed by Manny's hands.

This one's for you, Reg . . .

Reggie grabbed one of the handles on his casket and pulled, bringing the other end slamming into the ground before hauling the thing after him on the way to the exit. Now unsure of where to go, the younger crowd was trapped, unable to do anything but scream and cringe as far away as they could from the approaching ghoul.

Reggie lurched on, two members of the old crew brushing past him to hold the church doors open for his exit. When Clyde and Manny rose and started to follow, Clyde saw confusion begin to overtake those on the other side of the aisle. Still aghast but now well away from the danger, and with only one escape route available, they were forced to join the procession.

Clyde held his breath as Reggie hit the stairs. Despite the weight of the metal and electronics filling the husk, his old friend didn't even stumble while he made his way down, heading in the direction of the churchyard and the open grave that waited for him.

The screams were gone completely now, replaced by tense murmuring while the younger mourners followed the old guard out only to be trapped between walls of interlocked arms. Clyde fell into step a foot or two behind Reggie, flanked by Manny. Looking over his shoulder, he saw the rest of his crew stretch the barrier behind him, herding the crowd the rest of the way to their destination.

That's right. You're watching this through to the end.

Together, they made their way onto the grass and to the rows of tombstones in the back of the church. A pile of shovels waited graveside. This time, Clyde did sob when Reggie paused and thrust his burden into the waiting hole. Climbing in after the casket, he paused, turned, and bowed before giving a final wave and pulling open the door. Again inside, the coffin's hinges creaked as he sealed himself inside once more.

Rest easy, my friend.

Clyde picked up a shovel, each man after him taking it in turn to thrust the blade into the mound of earth and toss in a load. The crowd was pressed in close around them now, although the reverend was nowhere in sight. Already sore from days of prep work with the team, Clyde's back ached fiercely by the time the work was done. Yet, when he turned to his audience, he found something that made it all worthwhile. Something he knew neither he nor Reggie had earned in far too long: awe.

ACKNOWLEDGMENTS

Production of a book typically falls on more shoulders than merely those of the writer, and *Wind Chill* is no exception. So, now is the time to sing the praises of all the good folks who helped me get it out the gates.

First, I'd like to thank my beta reader extraordinaire Ben Eads who patiently suffers through all my dirty first drafts and manages to make them shine.

I'd also like to extend my regards to the folks at Crystal Lake Publishing. This goes out inparticular to Joe Mynhardt who saw potential enough in the book to publish it and gave itthe final spit polish it needed. Additional appreciation goes to Ben Baldwin who created one hell of a cover to wrap around my words.

As always, I also need to extend my gratitude to my family for their support. I know I'm as stubborn as they come, so thanks for putting up with me while I clack away at the keyboard like the lunatic I surely am.

Finally, I want to thank every one of you readers who spent time and money on my work.I hope it was worth the ticket price and to see you all again soon.

If you enjoyed this book, I'm sure you'll also like the following titles:

Eidolon Avenue: The First Feast—where the secretly guilty go to die. All thrown into their own private hell as every cruel choice, every deadly mistake, every drop of spilled blood is remembered, resurrected and relived to feed the ancient evil that lives on Eidolon Avenue.

The Outsiders Lovecraftian shared-world anthology—They'll do anything to protect their way of life. Anything. Welcome to Priory, a small gated community in the UK, where the only thing worse than an ancient monster is the group worshipping it. Is that which slithers below true evil, or does evil reside in the people of Priory? Includes stories by Stephen Bacon, James Everington, Rosanne Rabinowitz, V.H. Leslie, and Gary Fry.

Tales from The Lake Vol.1 anthology—Remember those dark and scary nights spent telling ghost stories and other campfire stories? With the *Tales from The Lake* horror anthologies, you can relive some of those memories by reading the best Dark Fiction stories around. Includes Dark Fiction stories and poems by horror greats such as Graham Masterton, Bev Vincent, Tim Curran, Tim Waggoner, Elizabeth Massie, and many more. Be sure to check out our website for future *Tales from The Lake* volumes.

Through a Mirror, Darkly by Kevin Lucia—Are there truths within the books we read? What if the book delves into the lives of the very town you live in? People you know? Or thought you knew. These are the questions a bookstore owner face when a mysterious book shows up.

Where You Live by Gary McMahon—Horror is everywhere, in the shadows and in the light. It takes on every shape, comes in every conceivable size. But most of all it's right where you live. With the WHERE YOU LIVE short story collection, Gary McMahon delves into the depths of dark and brooding horror in every day events, objects, and the ghost of human nature.

Samurai and Other Stories by William Meikle—No one can handle Scottish folklore with elements of the darkest horror, science fiction and fantasy, suspense and adventure like William Meikle.

If you ever thought of becoming an author, I'd also like to recommend these non-fiction titles:

The *Writers On Writing: An Author's Guide* Series— Your favorite authors share their secrets in the ultimate guide to becoming and being and author. With your support, *Writers On Writing* will become an ongoing eBook series with original 'On Writing' essays by writing professionals. A new edition will be launched every few months, featuring four or five essays per edition, Don, so be sure to check out the webpage regularly for updates.

Horror 101: The Way Forward—a comprehensive overview of the Horror fiction genre and career opportunities available to established and aspiring authors, including Jack Ketchum, Graham Masterton, Edward Lee, Lisa Morton, Ellen Datlow, Ramsey Campbell, and many more.

Horror 201: The Silver Scream Vol.1 and *Vol.2*—A must read for anyone interested in the horror film industry. Includes interviews and essays by Wes Craven, John Carpenter, George A. Romero, Mick Garris, and dozens more. Now available in paperback, as well.

Modern Mythmakers: 35 interviews with Horror and Science Fiction Writers and Filmmakers by Michael McCarty—Ever wanted to hang out with legends like Ray Bradbury, Richard Matheson, and Dean Koontz? *Modern Mythmakers* is your chance to hear fun anecdotes and career advice from authors and filmmakers like Forrest J. Ackerman, Ray Bradbury, Ramsey Campbell, John Carpenter, Dan Curtis, Elvira, Neil Gaiman, Mick Garris, Laurell K. Hamilton, Jack Ketchum, Dean Koontz, Graham Masterton, Richard Matheson, John Russo, William F. Nolan, John Saul, Peter Straub, and many more.

Or check out other Crystal Lake Publishing books for your Dark Fiction, Horror, Suspense, and Thriller needs.

BIOGRAPHY

Patrick Rutigliano made way as a fry cook, cart monkey, and feral cat tamer before going into business for himself. Working as an editor and proofreader in addition to writing, his first independent release, *The Untimely Deaths of Daryl Handy*, hit Amazon in 2013. His first novel, *Surviving the Crash*, was released by Retro Rocket Press in 2014.

During his off time, Patrick can usually be found attempting to recreate foreign cuisine, performing the solemn duty of feline waterbed, and having spirited debates with his wife over the failings of Disney villains.

CONNECT WITH THE AUTHOR

On Amazon:
http://www.amazon.com/Patrick-Rutigliano/e/B006WSAVUS

On Facebook:
https://www.facebook.com/patrick.rutigliano.author

On Twitter:
https://twitter.com/PatRutigliano

On Goodreads:
https://www.goodreads.com/author/show/4572968.Patrick_Rutigliano

Blog:
https://patrickrutigliano.wordpress.com

CONNECT WITH CRYSTAL LAKE PUBLISHING

Website (be sure to sign up for our newsletter):
www.crystallakepub.com
Facebook:
www.facebook.com/Crystallakepublishing
Twitter:
https://twitter.com/crystallakepub

With unmatched success since 2012, Crystal Lake Publishing has quickly become one of the world's leading indie publishers of Mystery, Thriller, and Suspense books with a Dark Fiction edge.

Crystal Lake Publishing puts integrity, honor and respect at the forefront of our operations.

We strive for each book and outreach program that's launched to not only entertain and touch or comment on issues that affect our readers, but also to strengthen and support the Dark Fiction field and its authors.

Not only do we publish authors who are legends in the field and as hardworking as us, but we look for men and women who care about their readers and fellow human beings. We only publish the very best Dark Fiction, and look forward to launching many new careers.

We strive to know each and every one of our readers, while building personal relationships with our authors, reviewers, bloggers, pod-casters, bookstores and libraries.

Crystal Lake Publishing is and will always be a beacon of what passion and dedication, combined with overwhelming teamwork and respect, can accomplish: Unique fiction you can't find anywhere else.

We do not just publish books, we present you worlds within your world, doors within your mind, from talented authors who sacrifice so much for a moment of your time.

This is what we believe in. What we stand for. This will be our legacy.

Welcome to Crystal Lake Publishing.

We hope you enjoyed this title. If so, we'd be grateful if you could leave a review on your blog or any of the other websites and outlets open to book reviews. Reviews are like gold to writers and publishers, since word-of-mouth is and will always be the best way to market a great book. And remember to keep an eye out for more of our books.

www.ingramcontent.com/pod-product-compliance
Lightning Source LLC
Chambersburg PA
CBHW070948190726
48292CB00004B/1372